MIKE'S MAGIC BURGERS

"Enjoy"

Mike's Magic Burgers

by Rose Baldwin

Rose Baldwin

SENESCERE

RANCHO MIRAGE, CALIFORNIA

Published 2017
Printed in the United States of America

ISBN: 978-0-9981390-1-2

Cover design: Challis & Roos
Cover photo: Dre Naylor
Interior formatted by Sunacumen Press, Palm Springs, CA

"Sonnet 43" by Elizabeth Barrett Browning was originally published as one of the "Sonnets from the Portuguese" in 1850 and is some-times referred to by the title "How do I Love Thee."

Prologue

Today Earl Witherspoon is rich and famous. But in the mid-1990s, he was just another guy who, along with me, hung out at Mike's Magic Burgers.

I've told his story here using information gathered from conversations with others who knew him, and from my own recollections—faulty though they may be. While putting the story together, I was struck by how much technology and security have changed since then, and how little people have.

Earl walked into Mike's in the middle of a midcareer upset. Though he mostly ignored the magic of the place, he was shown a way to make a difference in people's lives and used that opportunity to achieve enormous wealth and fame.

To be honest, I think the other people in Mike's were more interesting and have included some of their stories as well. You can decide for yourself.

Mike's Magic Burgers

Northern California's Best since 1965

M E N U

Tropical Burger — a pleasant walk on a warm sunny beach. (swimming is definitely allowed) relaxes your mind and refreshes your spirit.

Tropical Burger Deluxe — includes an encounter with a friendly local.

Oasis Burger — all the warmth and charm of the desert; relaxes and encourages appreciation for life.

Decision Burger — a knowledgeable expert always available to discuss your problems.

Fishy Burger — wet, warm, and friendly fun around a '55 Chevy.

Fishy Burger Deluxe — a little extra contact with the locals.

Betty's Business Burger — basic burger is the perfect business lunch. Can be served with one of three specialty sauces: Finance, Marketing, or Operations. All encourage honesty and forthrightness while sharpening business acumen and improving negotiating and presentation skills.

Tofu Burger — tastes good.

At Mike's Magic Burgers, the food and some of the people are magic.

Tropical Burger Deluxe

Daphne Miller's feet hurt as she stood in Mike's Magic Burgers, careful to keep her slim, silk-suited body away from the well-worn wooden counter where orders were taken. She was tired of waiting by the time a fifty-something-year-old man with a short buzz cut, plaid flannel shirt, faded jeans, and soiled apron appeared. His eyes sparkled, and he had an impish, deep-dimpled grin. In spite of her peevishness, she was captivated.

"Hi, sorry to keep you waiting," he said.

Daphne felt shy and confused about what to say. After a long pause, she managed, "My assistant suggested I come here. She told me to order Mike's Special Burger, but I don't see it on the menu. Oh, I almost forgot—I'm supposed to say, 'Blanche sent me.'"

"Is this your first time here?" he asked.

Daphne nodded. "Is this Mike's? Do you have a Special Burger?"

"I'm Mike." He smiled. "Do you like sunshine and beaches?"

"Sure," she said. Her captivation having evaporated, she added, "What does that have to do with anything?"

"I usually recommend the Tropical Burger for first-timers," he said. "The Special Burger is so delicious the bliss can be disorienting for someone unprepared." He smiled again.

This time his smile did not charm her. She was hungry. "So, you have a Special Burger that you won't sell to me because it's too delicious, and you want me to eat something not as good?"

"I'll tell you what. Since this is your first time, I'll *give* you a Tropical Burger—on the house." She made a frustrated hiss, and he added, "I'll make it a Deluxe. Find a seat. I'll bring it out."

She wanted to leave, but she had neither the time nor energy to find another restaurant. Resigning herself, she looked around. The decor (if anyone could call it that) was comprised of mismatched tables and chairs, and Naugahyde booths—some with duct-tape patches—on a floor of mismatched linoleum. The clientele was an unlikely mix of scruffy—almost dirty—people sitting next to suited professionals. An old woman sat in one corner reading palms.

Daphne chose a small booth near the front of the restaurant. Mike appeared at her side, before she'd even managed to warm the seat. Setting the plate with her burger on it in front of her, he cooed, "Enjoy," a habit she considered an annoying affectation. Cautious by nature, she lifted the sandwich with both hands and took a tiny bite. It was impossibly delicious! Taking a larger bite, she closed her eyes, and savored the remarkable flavor.

She was slightly dizzy and then felt warmth on her. Opening her eyes, she found herself on an expanse of white sand, looking out on a turquoise sea. The waves broke on the offshore reef, leaving only tiny surges on the beach. She saw a large man, dressed in white pants, carrying folded white towels and a basket with the pump tops of lotion bottles visible, walking toward her. Looking down, she realized that the platform she was sitting on, and had assumed was a chaise lounge, was really a massage table. She rolled onto her stomach, pulled the sheet over her, and waited.

She heard the pump of the oil and the sound of him rubbing it in his palms. Then he touched her. His hands were enormous, warm, and soft. He put one on her tailbone and the other at the base of her neck and made a small chant-like hum. Her body relaxed into a blissful calm. Slowly his powerful fingers dug into her back, tracing stiff muscles that burned then popped as they released their accumulated stress. Her mind wandered to another time and another beach as he massaged the backs of her legs, waking thighs too used to sitting for hours at a time.

She rolled onto her back.

He took her feet, which had suffered the indignity of high heels for decades, one at a time, rubbing and stretching them, working his powerful fingers into the soles. He pulled her toes and ran his finger between them, and she thought about what it had been like to be a child walking barefoot, in long cool grass.

Under his ministrations, the muscles in the front of her legs and then her arms released their stress, freeing a sweet song from her heart that brought tears to her eyes. Her keyboard-weary hands loosened; she moaned as he worked on her tired fingers, then stretched and rubbed each palm.

Finally, he probed the perpetually stiff muscles along her neck and then her face. After he finished, she lay for a long while, relishing the feel of sun on her body.

Opening her eyes, she was back in her small booth at Mike's, looking at an empty plate. Mike sat across from her. He spoke softly. "Was it okay?"

It took a moment for her to recognize him and remember where she was. She looked down at herself to make sure she was dressed (she was) and then around the room to see if people were staring (they weren't).

"Oh, yes," she said, then laughed at how deep and sensuous her voice sounded.

Mike reached across the table and touched her hand. "The Special Burger is a little stronger. You can have it next time, if you want."

"Thank you," she said.

Earl Witherspoon

Earl Witherspoon crossed the street, as he did every Friday after seeing his therapist, and entered Mike's Magic Burgers. "Hi, Mike," he said. "I'll have a double latte and biscotti."

He and Mike were the same age, but Mike looked years younger. Maybe it was that his jeans and plaid shirts, or, on warm days, T-shirts, made him look hip, while Earl's khakis and polo shirts seemed more adult. Or maybe Mike, with his muscled shoulders and arms, looked fit, and Earl, though not fat, did not. In the end, Earl decided Mike had simply lived an easy life—after all, he ran a burger joint—how hard could that be? Earl was an attorney; his job was hard and stressful. That's why he had to see Harvey, an expensive psychiatrist, every week.

Turning away from the counter, Earl caught the eye of the old woman sitting at a corner table behind the sign with 'Palms Read $10' printed on it. "Dee, want a lemonade?" he called out.

"Sure, Earl," she answered, pulling a second sign that read 'Out to Lunch' from behind her and placing it on the table. She stood to her full five-foot-ten-inch height, and strode across the room. Earl marveled at the contrast between the youthful grace of her movements and her weathered face that showed every minute of her eighty-three years. "Still wasting your money on that shrink?" she said. "You should pay me to read your palm instead."

"Business off?" he chided in return.

The two sat at the table by the window and Dee accepted the lemonade.

"It's the same every year at test time," Dee said. "The kids come in, wanting to know if they're going to pass."

Earl snickered. "What do you tell them?"

"That their fate is not yet sealed, and with sufficient effort and desire they can succeed," she said. "And if they don't, it may be an indication they are on the wrong path. That kind of stuff."

"What would you tell me?" Earl held his hand out, palm up.

"I didn't know you were a believer." She took his hand in hers, and cast him an inscrutable look. "I'd ask if you're sleeping all right."

"Actually, I'm not."

"Don't drink coffee so late in the day," she said, in an exaggerated sage tone.

Earl looked at the latte in front of him and laughed. "That it?" he asked.

"And I'd ask if you are suffering emotional turmoil."

"How did you get that?"

"This isn't rocket science." She shook her head. "You see a shrink every Friday. Why else would you do that?"

"Yeah, but what would you tell me to do about it?" he asked.

"Oh pffff," she said. "Usually turmoil just means it's time to take stock. Either learn to appreciate what you're doing or do something else."

"That's what the shrink says," Earl said. "But what am I supposed to do?"

"It's an opportunity." She shrugged. "Ignore it or embrace it."

"But…"

"How did you decide to become an attorney?" Dee asked. "How did you decide to marry your wife? How did you decide to have children? Earl, you know how to do this."

He nodded. "I became an attorney to help people. I thought I would help them follow the law and make smart decisions. And that was what my partners and I did in the beginning. It was good."

Dee nodded encouragement.

"I don't know when, but it changed. Our clients got mean and cheap, and truth be told, so did we—but only because we had to. Today my clients either want to pick a fight with someone they think can't afford to defend themselves, or they want to avoid paying taxes. We're paid to go along with it. We don't dare say a lawsuit is silly, that the legal fees will be more than they are likely to win—we follow orders. We're afraid some of them will sue us! It's frustrating."

Earl wished he could be this honest with Harvey. But the two of them belonged to the same country club, as did his partners and a fair number of his clients. He could say these things here. No one he knew ever came here.

"Our clients are fat, rich, selfish, and stingy. We sue over petty differences and argue over everything. They drive cars that cost more than a lot of houses and spend what most people live on every year for vacations in five-star resorts, where underpaid help cater to their whims and make them feel important. What I do doesn't make the world safer or more just or a better place in any way. It sure isn't what I dreamed of when I was in law school."

Feeling both relieved—to have final said these things out loud—and self-conscious, Earl stopped. "I'm sorry. I didn't mean to…I'm sorry."

Dee raised her hand. "I have that effect on people—probably my age. What does the shrink say?"

Earl didn't know what the shrink would say if he ever told him what he'd just told her, and he couldn't tell Dee that.

"He said what you said. Either learn to appreciate the good part of my work or do something else. But it's not that easy. I need the money. My older daughter is in medical school, and that's expensive. My wife likes our life and has no desire to change. Chic, the baby, is just finishing high school, then she goes to Berkeley—that won't be cheap. And what else would I do anyway?"

"What you're describing is exactly what it's like when destiny is trying to get your attention to remind you that you can do better."

"Destiny?" Earl said. "Really, Dee, that's a little far out for me."

"Oh, call it whatever you want," Dee said. "This is a time for you to reevaluate your life."

Earl shook his head. "That's what Harvey says, but he won't tell me what to do."

"Your discomfort is destiny's way of saying you have the opportunity to make a change. But you have to figure out what to do by yourself."

"I want to stop feeling anxious all the time. You know, I should be happy. I have everything I set out to get. Maybe if I ignore it, it will go away."

"If you do nothing, destiny might leave," Dee said. "But sometimes she doesn't. Sometimes she turns your world upside down and forces you to act."

Earl arched his eyebrow and chuckled. "That'd be something to see."

"It can be," Dee said in a serious tone.

An hour later, Earl drove his Mercedes into his garage and walked into his five- bedroom, midcentury-modern house in the hills overlooking the city. He heard an intense conversation coming from the patio and walked toward it.

Looking up, his friend Tom exclaimed, "Here's Earl. He'll settle it. Which grocery has a better selection of pâté, the one on the West side or Rio Del Mar?"

"I don't know what to say," Earl said.

"Why don't you admit you haven't been in either of them?" his wife, Beth, said, giving him a peck on the cheek and handing him a large glass of wine.

"Earl, you chauvinist. You don't shop? Ever?" Tom's wife, Jane, chortled. "Beth, you spoil him."

The three teased Earl while he quickly finished his wine and poured a second. The conversation shifted to where to get discounts on cashmere jackets and then domestic help. By the time Earl finished his second drink, he had begun to enjoy himself. By the end of the evening, he'd forgotten all about his angst. He thought he should find out about the market on the West side.

Betty's Business Burger

Next door to Mike's Magic Burgers was a gift shop that sold chicken-related items: chicken garden statues, pot holders and dish towels printed with chickens, T-shirts with chickens, pictures of chickens, mugs with chickens, and dishes with chickens. Anything you could think of to put a chicken on or make in the shape of a chicken, the little shop named Chicken Shit sold it. Maria de la Luz Lopez Washington Smithe, the shop's owner, ate at Mike's often. One day she came to the restaurant with a handsome, dark-haired, expensively suited gentleman in tow.

"Mike," Maria said, "this is Hinckley Harper, a vice president from First National Bank. I want to talk him into making me a loan, so I can expand my store. I thought a little magic might help."

"Nice to meet you, Mr. Harper." Mike looked from the banker in his dark, double-breasted suit over a blazing white shirt and subtly printed red tie, to Maria in her midcalf gauze skirt over leggings, wilted long-sleeved shirt, and beat-up Birkenstocks worn over thermal socks, and grinned.

"Has Maria explained that our burgers are magic?" he asked Hinckley. "They will help you explain yourself and understand others. They will also cause you to be honest and conduct yourself in good faith. Most people find the experience pleasant, but it can be disorienting for first-timers, especially if it's been a while since they've told the truth."

The banker nodded. "And then we go to a desert island, right?"

"No, that's another burger," Mike said. "There's only so much magic one burger can hold."

He turned to Maria. "Maria, do you understand that even with the help of magic, you may not be able to negotiate your loan?"

Her nod caused her abundant bosom to quake.

"Okay then," Mike said, "that's two Betty's Business Burgers with Finance Sauce. Sit anywhere you want. I'll bring out your food."

Maria wondered what Mike's silly grin had been about. She had business to do now but could come back later and ask—maybe it was some interesting gossip.

Settling at a table, the banker opened his briefcase and removed several typed pages, a yellow pad, and a gold Cross pen. Maria took the pack off her back and removed her own yellow pad and a ballpoint pen with the name of a local tire store on the side.

"Enjoy," Mike said, setting a burger in front of each

of them. Maria lifted hers, closed her eyes, and took a large bite, as she always did when eating at Mike's. Hinckley Harper followed her lead.

Opening her eyes, Maria saw Hinckley's unbankerly grin. "Are you okay, Mr. Harper?"

"This is really a great burger," he said. "Please, call me Hinckley." Smiling coyly, he added, "Maria." Then, "Oh! Did I say that out loud?"

Maria felt herself blush. "It's the burger talking. Don't worry about it. If you don't mind, I'd like to get right down to business. As you know, I plan to take over the empty space next to my existing store—approximately tripling my size. I'll change the name to Animal World. Popular animals will each have their own department; Bunny Hutch, Bear Cave, and of course to honor the original store, Chicken Shit."

The banker lifted the typed notes he'd brought with him. "The bank is uncomfortable because your store is too specialized. It is difficult for us to believe there are enough people who want to buy this kind of…"

"Junk?" Maria said, and he nodded.

"I've been open for ten years and profitable from day one. The expansion will diversify my business." Maria spoke with confidence even though she was finding the banker's smile distracting. It was a nice smile, sweet and slightly lopsided. She'd never noticed it before.

"Let me continue," the banker said. "I admire the way you run your business. But the loan is outside our normal parameters. It's too big for me to make on my own and too small to be of much interest to the rest of the bank. I personally have no doubt you'll do well and repay. But the bank requires two signatures on a loan this size, and I just can't find anyone to sign off with me."

Normally the magic would have kept her on topic. But today Maria was distracted by the realization that she and Hinckley were about the same age. She had to work to push that thought aside.

"What if I intend to ask for more money?" She reached into her backpack and took out a three-ring binder with *Animal World Business Plan* written across the front. "What if the expansion is only the first step? What if I have a plan to open a chain of stores?"

Hinckley's look was dreamy, but his words were all business. "Where will the equity come from?"

"I've prepared this folder for potential investors. My first step is to expand this store. I hope to have the physical work completed by September, so I'll be ready for Christmas. Assuming holiday sales are strong, I feel certain a private investor will step up, and together we'll open five stores and prepare for a public offering. With the first offering, we'll cover the region. Based on that performance, we can do a large offering and go national. It's all here—projections, plans, industry comparisons." She pushed the binder toward him.

"Has anyone committed?" he asked.

"Letters of intent are in the back of the binder," Maria said. "There are three potential investors. They all like the concept but expect me to make the initial improvements—so they can see how the expanded store performs through the peak shopping season. You can see the people are reputable and the proposed investments substantial."

Hinckley read the letters. "I can sell this." He looked pleased, and then there was that something else—a softness, a hopefulness.

She looked into his brown eyes and thought, *Not now! Damn it, not now!* but felt the fuzzy-ball-in-the-stomach-feeling of first attraction in spite of her efforts.

"Oh!" Hinckley said, opening his eyes, a clean plate on the table in front of him.

Mike was standing next to the table. "Any good?" he asked.

"Yeah," Hinckley and Maria both said, not looking at each other.

Maria didn't need to ask Mike what he had been grinning about earlier. She wondered how he knew these things before anyone else.

Meditate

Dee was sitting at the window table of Mike's Magic Burgers reading a letter when Earl walked into the restaurant. He ordered their usuals, carried them to where she sat, and joined her.

"Earl. Hi," Dee said, accepting the lemonade. "Make another payment on your shrink's Porsche?"

"Yeah, I guess I did." He gestured toward the letter. "Did you get bad news? You look a little glum."

"Sort of. My daughter just finished a cookbook."

"How is that bad news?" Earl asked.

"Oh, that's the good part. The bad part is every time she finishes a book, she changes her life. Moves. I'm worried she's never going to settle."

"How many books has she written?"

"Five."

Earl felt himself wince. He'd lived in only four different places in his whole life.

Dee patted his hand. "Earl, not everyone decides on a career in high school, marries his college sweetheart, and lives happily ever after in the town his family settled. Dee Dee's lived all over the world, speaks several languages passably. It's an exciting life. But I'm her mother. I want to see her settled."

Earl smiled. "Your daughter's name is Dee Dee? Like, Dee's daughter?"

Dee nodded. "It seemed like a good idea at the time. And no, my granddaughter is not named Three-Dee." She paused briefly, and then added, "We didn't have the glasses."

It was Earl's sort of humor, and he gave a nod of appreciation.

"She goes to foreign places? Other countries? How can she do that?" He hoped the questions seemed like curiosity, engagement, not the incredulity he actually felt.

"I've never understood it," Dee admitted. "Dee Dee is drawn to a place. She immerses herself in the language, culture, and ideas. A big part of being anywhere is getting used to the local foods. She writes down recipes as she learns them and adds stories she hears, local legends, poems—that's the book."

"Dee, that sounds like a wonderful life! I could never do something like that." He didn't want to admit that even the thought of travel to anywhere English wasn't spoken scared him. "Lawyers aren't that mobile—and I have a wife and family. Hasn't Dee Dee ever found a place she wanted to stay?"

"The way she explains it," Dee said, "finishing the

book feels like the end of a party, as if it's time to leave. She tried to stay a couple of times, but it didn't work. Once the house she was living in burned down. Another time her day job evaporated—the company just decided they didn't need that job done anymore."

"So she believes in destiny, too?" Earl said.

Dee smiled and nodded.

"I've been thinking about what you told me," Earl said. "What if destiny really is a thing, and it's calling me? Let's say, I decide to be an artist. What would I do about money? How would I support myself?"

"I don't know," Dee said. "But somehow, you would. It's interesting how obstacles disappear."

"Yeah, right," Earl scoffed.

"Too airy-fairy for you?"

Earl nodded. "Even though being an attorney isn't as satisfying as it once was, I don't know of anything I'd rather do. How would I even come up with something?"

"You could meditate or do yoga," Dee said. "Either one will give you a chance to hear from destiny, and they're great for relaxation."

"Harvey says the same thing—not about destiny, but about relaxing. He says I need to learn to appreciate my good fortune."

"I agree." Dee laughed.

He smiled amiably, though he was tired of people telling him to meditate and do yoga. He was an attorney. He worked with laws and facts, not this feel-good mumbo jumbo.

❖

Earl went from Mike's Magic Burgers to the art museum to attend the opening of a new show. He saw his wife, Beth, as soon as he entered the main gallery. She was one of the tallest women there, almost as tall as he, and still slim. Her style was casual, and she wore her short hair tousled. She was at the far side of the room, engaged in a rapid-fire conversation, with another woman. He wondered what had inspired their passion.

Approaching, he heard Beth's companion say, "Did you see the silk sweaters? They were marked down 60 percent. I bought three!"

"No! I missed them," Beth said. "Were there many left? Think it's worth my time to try tomorrow?"

Beth looked up at Earl's approach. "Earl! This is Pat. She was just telling me about the sweaters on sale at Magnin. Can you imagine? I was there this afternoon and missed them."

Earl picked up the beat immediately. "Maybe you can get them tomorrow—if you go early in the morning."

"Yes, darling. Is there anything you need?" Beth asked. "We can go together. What fun, uh?"

Earl thought of his dresser drawers full of socks, underwear, and sweaters, and his closet full of suits, shirts, slacks, and blazers, and he wondered if he would ever really need to buy another stitch of clothing as long as he lived.

"I think I'll go look at the show," he said.

"Go ahead. We've already seen it," Beth said. "It's that guy who paints with his body parts. This is the right-knee series. I thought the left-elbow series was better."

As he walked away, Earl heard her return to her conversation. "How about housewares? I have a large upright mixer and a little handheld, but I could use one in between. Were they on sale?"

Oasis Burger

Phil Reardon stomped his feet on the mat just outside Mike's Magic Burgers, opened the door, and bellowed, "Hi-ho! Mike." Once at the order counter, he sang out, "An Oasis Burger, if you please, or even if you don't. After all, I'm eating it." Then he laughed at his oft-repeated joke.

Mike smiled and nodded.

Working his way to his favorite booth, Phil greeted friends and strangers alike.

"Good afternoon."

"Hey there."

"Nice day."

"Haven't seen you in a while!"

"Good-looking shirt—where can I get one?"

As he settled into his seat, Mike brought his food, and Phil roared a hearty "Thank you." He lifted the sandwich with both hands, closed his eyes, and took a large bite. He felt the heat on him and smiled. Then he opened his eyes on a panoramic view of a desert—miles and miles of nothing.

The mountains were behind him. He turned to look up a canyon and could see a hint of green that was the palm trees of the oasis in the distance. The temperature was a dry ninety-five degrees. As he walked up the hill, his breathing deepened, and his husky body began to sweat.

He loved the desert. The plants growing out of rock crevices displayed the ultimate tenacity of life. That they could also produce flowers left him dizzy with delight. Along his walk he inspected each plant. Wary of thorns and stickers, he carefully held his hand just short of touch. He loudly sang tuneless songs to them. "Oh, agave; oh, agave, majestic century plant!"

He looked at the brush high up along the side of the canyon to where some coyotes lived. Two pups were playing, and he stopped to watch. The mother came out from behind a bush and eyed him suspiciously.

"Don't worry, Mama. I won't hurt your babies."

He went on, "Oh *Fouquieria spendens*—may I call you ocotillo? I await your red flowers."

A small lizard scurried across his path, and he stopped to watch and said, "Gosh, you're fast. Almost didn't see you."

Moving on, he began to sing again, "Oh, hedgehog cactus, with your pretty pink blooms. Behold the miracle of life!"

At the oasis, there was a ring of palm trees with a pool of water in the center. He removed his sweat-soaked clothes, walked into the shallow water, dropped to his knees, and then belly flopped forward, causing water to cascade up around the sides of the pool. Floating up from the bottom, he felt the sun on his wet, naked back. He raised his head and yelled, "Yes, this is the life!" with all his might.

Mike's smiling face greeted him when he opened his eyes. "Batch okay?"

"Any way to make that walk longer? It's over too fast," Phil said. "Oh, the coyote had her litter. I saw two pups."

Time Alone

Friday afternoon, after an appointment with his therapist, Earl stood in Mike's Magic Burgers studying the menu mounted behind the order counter. After more time than it took most people to decide, he told Mike, "I'll try an herbal tea."

"Biscotti?"

Earl nodded.

Dee appeared suddenly, as she sometimes did. "Quit drinking coffee in the afternoon?" she asked Earl.

"Oh! Where did you come from?" Earl said, startled. "Yeah, I'm trying some herbal tea. Thanks for the suggestion to cut out the afternoon coffee. I'm sleeping better."

Earl shifted impatiently from foot to foot. "I'm glad you're here, Dee. I've got to tell someone what Harvey told me today. He said I should go away for a while and rethink my life."

"That sounds like a good idea," Dee said. "Let's go sit down."

Earl talked as they walked, chose a table and sat. "I haven't been away from my wife for longer than three days since we got married twenty-five years ago. What would she think?"

Dee shrugged. "I don't know. What would she think?"

"What do you think she'd think if I walked in and said, 'Hi honey, Doc suggests I need to get away, see ya?' What would my work partners say?"

"Earl, he didn't just say, 'get away.' What came first?" Dee asked, "Start at the beginning."

"I tried meditating and doing some breathing exercises, but I just couldn't do them. I told him I got distracted, and he said if I couldn't find a half hour a day to do something just for myself, I was overcommitted. That I should get away, rethink my priorities, and look for ways to simplify my life.

"So I said, 'Beth and I are going away for the weekend.' And he said, 'Two or three days may not be enough,' and anyway I should go by myself. What am I going to do?"

Dee shook her head. "Whatever you want."

"You don't understand," Earl said. His lips were pursed. "If I don't go, it will mean I'm paying someone to give me advice that I ignore. That would be stupid."

"Then go," Dee said.

"What will Beth think?" Earl whined.

"Earl, people go away all the time. She probably won't think anything."

"I just can't believe she wouldn't be upset," Earl said.

Earl almost tripped over the suitcase that sat by the door when he got home. Beth walked toward him, phone to her ear. "I'll take the red-eye and meet you at the hospital in the morning." After a brief pause, she said, "I love you too," and ended the call.

"Hi sweetie. I wasn't sure where to reach you. Mom's in the hospital. They're doing tests. She may need bypass surgery. Dad sounds lost. I have to go. A car is coming to take me to the airport."

"Do you want me to go with you?" Earl asked.

"If you want, but it's not necessary. With luck, it'll only be a few days. I haven't spent any time alone with my parents in years. This will give us a chance to have those famous parent-child talks."

Earl wondered if destiny had made Beth's mother sick so he would be alone but then dismissed the idea as hooey. Watching Beth gather her things, he realized he was angry that she felt so free to leave. Not that she shouldn't go—of course she should. These were her parents; they were getting older, and they may have things to discuss. But when Harvey had told him to take some time alone, he'd worried about Beth and what she'd think. She hadn't even talked with him before planning to go to her mother. Then he wondered what they'd talk about—what she would say about him.

His daughter Chic was on a ski trip with friends from school, so he was going to really be on his own. He had some work from the office, and there was a book he wanted to read; that and the Sunday paper and football were enough to keep him busy for the weekend. He missed having people around and was relieved when Beth called Saturday evening saying she'd be home in less than a week.

By Monday Earl was looking forward to the camaraderie at work. The flashing lights of fire trucks, emergency response vehicles, and police cars that confronted him when he pulled into his office parking lot distressed him. He drove to the space marked with his name. His partner sat with the top of his BMW convertible down in the space next to his.

Earl climbed out of his car. "Fire?" he asked.

"Quarantine. Five people from the insurance agency on the floor above ours are in the hospital with an as yet undiagnosed disease. That older woman—the heavy one who's always so happy—may not make it."

As other workers arrived, the story was told and retold. It became clear there was nothing to do but take the day off when authorities said they didn't expect to have anything to report until evening.

The people around him looked delighted to have an unplanned holiday, but Earl was dismayed. He'd managed to get through the weekend alone, but what was he going to do on a weekday if he didn't work? He comforted himself by thinking that if he could get through this, then maybe Harvey would move on and tell him what he needed to do to feel satisfied.

No one was allowed to enter the building for two more days. In spite of his initial trepidation, Earl enjoyed the time off. He wandered around the mall, visited a museum, went to a movie, and read a spy novel—he even managed to do the breathing exercises Harvey had shown him and a brief meditation. Now maybe Harvey would give him what he wanted.

He didn't need therapy—really—he only needed someone to tell him what was wrong.

A First Date

John had been to Mike's Magic Burgers for special lunches with the other mechanics who worked at Steve's garage. Steve treated them well, and jobs in his shop were valued. Most of them were older men.

John's father had worked there before he'd left town, leaving his then ten-year-old son and his mother to fend for themselves. When it was time for John to go to college, his mother had asked Steve to give him a job so he could pay his college tuition. Steve agreed to give it a try and even found John some secondhand coveralls—that *Chuck* was embroidered over the pocket didn't concern anyone. While his employment had started as a favor, Steve now said John was the best natural mechanic he'd ever met.

The first time John went to the restaurant in the evening, was when he brought Catherine. He'd cleaned up for the occasion; he'd scrubbed under his nails, gotten a haircut, and even shaved, though he only had a few hairs that might be called whiskers and didn't actually need to yet. Mike looked at the couple and gave John the universal guy-to-guy look of appreciation. John saw it and nodded. Catherine was beautiful, a red-haired athlete. Though John appreciated her looks, he was with her because she was nice and smart.

"Hey, John, my man, you look great," Mike said. "Who's with you?"

John felt his face redden. "Catherine, this is Mike. He owns this restaurant."

Catherine extended her hand, and John watched Mike react to her firm grip.

"John, how come you never told me about Catherine?"

"This is our, ah, first date. You know, we've known each other a long time—a real long time—but this is our first, uh, you know, first real, date." John shifted his weight. "Ah, we'd like two Special Burgers."

Mike gave John a sidelong look. "Catherine, you go pick a table. John and I are going to discuss the menu." He waited until she was out of earshot and whispered, "John, you know the rules; no Special Burgers on the first date. Have Tropical Burgers—everyone likes them."

John objected. "Aw, Mike, I was hoping for more than a walk on the beach. Know what I mean?"

"I know very well what you mean," Mike said softly to the boy.

Having grown up without a father, John worried he didn't know about manly things. He could see in Mike's eyes that he was going to get some fatherly advice. Steve sometimes gave him the same look. Though the advice annoyed him, John usually followed it.

"Listen to me," Mike said. "This is important. It will soil your soul forever if you trick a woman into doing something she might not actually want to do. Heck, it will soil you no matter who you trick—though I doubt you're in the mood to have that conversation right now. But listen, I know what I'm talking about."

Mike nodded toward Catherine. "She looks like she could be a keeper. You especially don't rush things with a keeper—things will happen soon enough. If you rush, it can ruin everything between you forever."

Before John could form an argument, Mike ended the conversation. "Anyway John, rules are rules. No Special Burgers for first-timers or on the first date."

Tropical Burgers it was.

Catherine had chosen the table by the window. The couple talked and looked out to the street until Mike delivered their food. John was relieved that Mike had made the decision for him. He wanted Catherine to like him. He didn't want to make a mistake.

Mike delivered the sandwiches with the usual admonition to "Enjoy."

Seeing the sandwiches, John worried that Catherine might not think the burgers were special enough, and he wondered if they should have gone to a fancy restaurant, even though he couldn't really afford it.

Catherine smiled and lifted her burger to her nose with both hands and sniffed. "Smells good," she said. She took a tiny nibble, and her face lit up. She closed her eyes and took a larger bite.

Seeing her, John was relieved and took a bite of his burger. The two met on the beach. It was warm and sunny, a welcome relief from the cold damp of Northern California, and they went for a swim. Then they lay on the sand absorbing the warmth for a long time before they returned.

Catherine and John looked up from their plates at each other. Mike was waiting. "Was it okay?" Mike asked.

"Where did that bathing suit come from?" Catherine asked. "I want one just like it. It was the most comfortable suit I've ever worn."

"That's how you know it's magic," Mike said. "Real bathing suits are never that comfortable."

"How come we had suits?" John asked. "When I've gone before, I didn't have one."

"Yeah, there's a suit when there should be," Mike said. "Funny how the magic always knows."

Beth Comes Home

Earl bypassed the order counter and went straight to the rear of Mike's Magic Burgers where Dee sat, behind her 'Palms Read $10' sign, deep in thought.

"Oooohmmmm," he said, bowing with his hands together. Then he slid into the chair across from her. "I've just had the most remarkable week. I was alone, and I did fine. I went to the mall, saw a movie, read a book, and even managed to meditate—I feel great."

"That's wonderful, Earl," Dee said.

"Guess Harvey was right. I was overcommitted and needed some time to myself. Now I can move on to other stuff."

"Have you seen Harvey?" Dee asked.

"He's on vacation. But I feel wonderful."

"Earl, I think he may want you to…"

"No," Earl said, bringing his hand down on the table. "He said I should be alone and I was. I was overcommitted. See?"

"Earl, obligations change but commitments don't go away. Commitments are life," Dee said. "You had a vacation—that's all."

"I'm a professional." Earl's voice rose in pitch and volume. "I have a wife and family. I can't change that."

"That's my point," Dee said. "Your life is the same."

Earl was frustrated. "I did what you and Harvey said. Now what do you want?"

"I'm just saying there may be more to it."

"What do you mean?" Earl's voice squeaked. "He said be alone, and I was."

Dee leaned back her and raised her hands. "I want to encourage you, but I feel like I'm in over my head here and real close to making an enemy. You need to discuss this with your shrink, not a palm reader."

Beth saw Earl bouncing with glee as she exited the Jetway. He ran forward hugged her, and kissed her. "I missed you so much."

"Sorry, Earl," she said, pulling away from him. "Our takeoff was delayed, we sat on the plane a long time, a woman behind me got sick, and there was a crying child a few seats over. All I want is to go home and take a hot bath."

Seeing his disappointment, she leaned in and kissed him on the cheek. "I'm sorry to be like this. I missed you too, sweetie."

If she hadn't been so grateful for the quiet, Beth

might have felt bad that Earl sulked during the drive home. She went straight from the car to the bathroom and filled the tub. Lowering herself into the hot water, she felt the weariness from the past week rise in her with a rush of emotions and she cried.

Her parents had gotten old. Her mother looked tiny and fragile lying in that hospital bed. Her pale skin and white hair blended into the white of the sheets. Her father, who had always been so vital, had grown thin and frail. Why was this the first time she'd noticed? It hadn't been that long since she'd seen them.

Reclining in the tub, she looked down at her own body and, for the first time, noticed the bulges of middle age. This was not just ten extra pounds. Her body had the first signs of old-lady crepey skin over fat. She added more hot water and cried some more. By the time she got out of the tub, Earl had gone to bed, leaving her to continue her thoughts and tears, alone.

When Earl woke the next morning, he was still angry. He had so much to tell Beth. How could she act like that? He'd wanted to tell her how he'd gone to the mall and a movie all by himself—how he felt like a new man—and all she wanted to do was take a bath. God, she was insensitive. It infuriated him that she lay sleeping soundly. "Well," he thought, "she could have the whole day to take all the baths she wanted." He went to his office.

Nirvana Burger

By the time Daphne Miller returned to Mike's Magic Burgers, she'd dismissed the idea that the sauce had been magic and transported her to a desert island. Obviously, such a thing couldn't happen. When she came last time, she'd been tired and hungry. The name Tropical Burger had suggested a daydream to her—that's all. She could allow that the burger had been delicious, and that's just what she wanted now. She was pleased when Mike recognized her.

"Hi, you're back." Mike flashed his wonderful smile. "Great. I'm trying a new recipe. I think it'll be called the Nirvana Burger because it's such a heavenly experience. Willing to try it? You'll be one of the first."

Daphne thought a heavenly experience was just what she needed. "Sure," she said.

By the time she'd gotten comfortable in the same small booth where she'd sat the first time, Mike was standing next to her. His admonition to "Enjoy" didn't seem nearly as annoying as the first time.

Looking down at the sandwich, she was glad she'd come. She woke up with a taste for a burger this morning and the hours had dragged as she waited for lunchtime to come. She picked up the warm sandwich in both hands, closed her eyes, and took a large bite.

Opening her eyes, she saw a tall figure wearing a hooded, floor-length, white satin cape with white feathers floating in the air around it. She noticed the graceful hands, with their long tapered fingers and shiny buffed nails. The figure's face was hidden in the shadow of the hood.

The cape opened. She stepped in and laid her head on the broad shoulder in front of her. Strong arms wrapped the cape tightly around her, and she felt the pink satin lining on her as she and the mystery figure began spinning. She wrapped her arms and legs around the caped figure, and they tumbled as if caught in a large wave.

As they spun, she surrendered her will, letting the two of them merge into one. As the tumbling continued, she saw scenes from her past and visions she thought could be the future.

A tingling lightness, like giggles, spread over her body as she looked on a sky-blue sea of nothingness. She felt, rather than saw, hints of pink, yellow, and pale green. She turned her head to one side then the other, trying to catch a glimpse of them, laughing when she didn't. She looked out into the surrounding expanse and felt the beckoning of invisible white tufts that she somehow knew were just beyond the empty blue sky, and she reached out to them with her heart.

A pulsing sensation started at the base of her belly and moved up through her like waves of energy, sending fireworks into the sky to rain back down on her. It grew stronger, then faster. When she could endure the ecstasy no longer, she closed her eyes and felt the rhythmic merging of her body and soul into the pulse of the universe.

Opening her eyes, she saw Mike's concerned face. "Too much summer savory?"

"Not that I noticed," she said, her voice low and sensuous.

Bill's Retiring

Beth sat at her dining room table, college catalogs and brochures spread out in front of her. She'd thought she had at least another half hour before she had to straighten up and start dinner, and was surprised to hear the garage door open, a car pull in, and then the door close noisily. Earl walked in through the back door.

"You're home early," she said.

"Yeah, I didn't stop after my session." Earl gestured at the jumble of paper. "Wow what a mess! Are you helping Chic find a school? I really think she should do this on her own, Beth. You can help a little, but it looks as if you're doing all of it. Besides, I thought she already decided to go to Berkeley."

"It's not for her. It's for me."

"What?" Earl said. "What are you talking about? You have a degree."

"Ever since I saw Mom," Beth said, "I've been so

aware of time passing and things not done. Do you know Mom always wanted to go to Paris? She used to talk about it when I was a little girl. While I was sitting with her in the hospital, she turned to me and said, 'Guess I'm not going to see the Eiffel Tower.' I felt so sad for her. It was the only thing she ever really wanted. I always wanted to teach. Since the girls are grown..." Beth looked up at Earl. Seeing he looked angry, she stopped.

"This is the first I've heard about this," he said.

She'd been dreading this conversation. "I'm still thinking about it," she said, hoping it didn't sound like the lie it was.

"You don't need to work," Earl said. "Why do you want to do this? Everything will change. You won't be here. Everything's changing."

"Earl, you're busy with your work. What difference does it make if I go back to school?"

"Bill's retiring," Earl said quickly.

Beth was quiet. What was the connection there between Bill retiring and her going to school? She and Earl had been married a long time, but she still had to remind herself to slow down and figure out what his concerns were. Lately, she'd become annoyed that he never did the same for her. Never.

"Will that mean a change at the office?" she asked, thinking it was a safe comment.

"Of course it will!" he snapped. "It will change everything."

Beth felt her stomach tighten in anger.

Earl gave an exasperated puff and stomped out of the room, leaving her to clear the table. She stacked the catalogs, careful to put those from out-of-state schools on the bottom. Then she made dinner, picturing herself away from here—at school. Sitting in a lecture hall taking notes, running through the halls between classes.

Her daydream was interrupted by the phone. Answering it, she heard Bill's voice, "So? What do you think?"

"Earl just told me you were retiring. Is there more?"

"We're going sailing!" Bill sounded excited. "We've wanted to for years. Joined a cruising club. Read the books and magazines. Learned Morse code. We want to go while we're still strong and healthy enough to enjoy ourselves. We think we may even be able to sail around the world."

"Oh, Bill, that's wonderful," Beth said. "I'm so happy for you."

"Is he there?"

She covered the mouthpiece, yelled for Earl, and hung up once he was on the line. By the time he'd finished talking and come into the kitchen, she was putting dinner on the table.

Earl sat in his usual place at the head of the table. "What do you think?" he said.

"I think it's wonderful," Beth said. "He said they'd planned for years and that they wanted to go while they were still strong. I talked with his wife about cruising at the Christmas party, but I had no idea they were this serious."

"Don't you think he's young to retire?" Earl said, fussily rearranging the food on his plate.

"It sounds like they think it's better to retire young

than to try to sail old."

"If he changes his mind, he'll never get his earnings back up where they are now," Earl said. "He'll be too old. Things change. Even a year out of the business, and he'll never come back. I don't think he realizes what he's doing.

"We'll have to replace him," Earl said. "It won't be easy. The four of us have worked together more than twenty years. Maybe he'll change his mind. What a mess."

Earl mixed his vegetables and potato together. He cut his meat and alternated bites of the potato/vegetable mixture with a bite of meat. He worked hard to ensure they always came out even.

Beth ate quietly, envying Bill and his wife for having a common goal. She knew if she said anything more to Earl now it would start a fight, and she wasn't up for it. Let him blow off steam. Maybe give him a drink or two. He'd settle down and go to bed early, leaving her to her own thoughts, which had, lately, been very full.

It Needs Salt

Maria walked into Mike's Magic Burgers carrying a cloth shopping bag with fresh herbs sticking out the of the top and yelled, "Hey, guy, things are going well in my world. I took a vacation day. Dee asked me to bring these to you—she's taking the day off too. What's up with you?"

Mike came out of the kitchen.

"What is it, Mike?" Maria asked. "You look as if you're carrying the weight of the world." She set the bag on the order counter and opened her arms to hug him.

"I've got a new recipe; it's good, but I think the summer savory is off," Mike said. "Would you taste it?"

"Sure," Maria said. "What are you going to call it?"

Mike spoke distractedly. "Nirvana Burger—because it's a heavenly experience."

She sat in her usual place. Mike brought her burger and set it in front of her. Instead of his usual "Enjoy" and seamless departure, he started to sit across from her.

She shushed him away with her hand. "Oh no, you're not going to sit there staring at me. Go back to the kitchen. I'll tell you what I think."

He walked toward the kitchen but stopped at the counter. From there he watched as she held the burger in both hands and took a bite. She frowned slightly. Then she a made quizzical look, then broke into a broad smile. As she ate, her face registered delight, amazement, bliss, and finally, satisfaction.

He waited until she opened her eyes before he went back to her table. "Well?" he said, afraid of what she would tell him.

"Needs salt," she said.

"I don't use salt."

"It needs salt. Just a little," she said. "Without it the summer savory is left out there a little too much on its own. Try a half teaspoon per batch."

Mike nodded. "That's what the recipe said."

"Why did you leave it out?"

"I don't use salt," Mike said.

"Why do you use the recipe if you're not going to follow it?"

"So it tastes good."

"Fine, then add the salt."

"I don't use salt."

Maria laughed. "Well, Mike, you have a decision to make. The name is great, and it is a heavenly experience. But it needs salt."

"Maria, this is the sort of thing my customers deal with."

"Yeah, that's why it's funny. What would you say to one of them?"

"I'd ask if it would really hurt to add a tiny bit to the sauce."

"Right. What's the answer?"

"I don't use salt. The decision was made so long ago I can't remember why I made it—but I am still committed to it."

Maria stood up and hugged Mike. "Change is hard. It needs salt."

Swindell, Dodge, and Armbruster

As usual, Friday afternoon Earl stood at the order counter of Mike's Magic Burgers.

"Herbal tea?" Mike asked.

"No. That stuff tastes like dishwater. Give me a double latte and biscotti. Make it decaf." He looked toward the back of the restaurant. Seeing that Dee was at her palm reader's table, he added, "And a lemonade."

He carried the drinks to her and sat down.

"You look tired," she said. "Everything okay?"

Earl put his hand, palm up, on the table. "You tell me."

She studied the palm. Her face grew serious, and she looked up. "You must feel very confused if you're ready to start believing in palm reading. You know it's not real. Right?"

"Dee, everything is changing," Earl said. "I feel out of control."

"Maybe this is the just the first time things didn't go the way you planned."

Earl told her Bill was retiring and that Beth was thinking about going back to school. Worse yet, his remaining partners were ready to merge with another law firm he did not like.

"I can't do this, Dee. I've lost a lot of my enthusiasm for work, but I still do a good job. I'm still proud of the service I provide. Swindell, Dodge and Armbruster are sleazy. They make money, and it's all legal. But I can't practice their kind of law."

"What's wrong with them? A friend of mine used them and was very happy."

"Dee, they advertise on television!"

"So?"

"That is just a different sort of law."

"But don't they provide legal services to people who might otherwise not know who to call?"

"Yes. But they do a lot of contingency work."

"Didn't you say you missed working with regular people?"

"You don't understand."

"No, I don't," Dee said. "But okay. What are your choices?"

"Stay or go," Earl said. "I tried to talk my partners out of the merger. There are only three of us voting and the other two favor it. We'll make more money, have better facilities, and won't work any harder than we do now. They're determined to do it."

"What does the shrink say?" Dee asked.

"You know he really never says much." Earl could

hear the peevishness in his comment. He was growing tired of these weekly sessions that seemed to achieve nothing. Harvey was supposed to be good. Earl wondered why, after all these months, Harvey still hadn't made his problems go away.

"He asked me what I wanted to do. Like, 'Earl, what are your choices?' And I said, 'Stay or go.' And he said, 'So it's one or the other.' And I said, 'How can I choose?' And he said, 'Flip a coin.' And I said, 'This is my life,' but I flip the coin and it comes up stay, and I say, 'I can't.' And he said, 'Well then, the decision is made.' Like it's that easy. What will I do?"

"Is there another firm in town you could work for? Is there something different that you've always wanted to try?" Dee asked.

Earl shook his head. "I never considered it, Dee. I thought I'd be a lawyer until I was too old to work. Then I'd take a trip or two, to make Beth happy, maybe go to Paris—she'd like that. Then I'd die. I'm too old to join another firm or do anything new. But I'm too young to die."

Dee shook her head. "This is what I tried to tell you. Once things start to change, there can just be a cascade of events. People face this all the time. You can call it destiny or whatever else you want. But whatever you call it, it helps if you consider this an opportunity."

Earl moaned. "Make it go away."

Dee said, "Still meditating?"

"Can't. Too upset," Earl said.

"Do. It helps."

Earl rocked slightly. "I can't do anything new. I'm

too old. There isn't enough time."

"Oh, Earl, you're only in your fifties," Dee said. "You have plenty of time."

Earl's lip trembled—he was close to tears. Dee took his hand in hers, and looking intently at his palm she said, "After a period of great upheaval you will have joy and satisfaction beyond your dreams."

Earl pulled back his hand. "This isn't a joke!"

"No one is laughing. I'm trying to be nice. I know this isn't easy for you."

Earl glared. "I don't want to do this."

"I see that."

Earl, who was used to having someone waiting for him, began talking as soon as he opened the back door to his house.

"I've had a terrible day," he said. "The firm is merging with Swindell. I can't work with those guys. The other partners are in favor of it; it's only me against, so it's a done deal. I'm going to the cottage for a of couple days to think about what to do."

Beth sat on the sofa, staring at a letter that lay, on the coffee table in front of her. She did not acknowledge Earl.

"Beth, are you listening to me?"

"Yes." Beth said, still staring at the letter. "I think that's a good idea. Go to the cottage for a of couple days and think about what to do."

"This is important," Earl said, his voice rising. "I'm

talking about changing my career. You don't seem to understand how important that is. I have to reevaluate everything, and you're not paying attention."

"You're right," Beth said, finally looking up. "I'm not paying attention. I was accepted at Berkeley, and I've decided I'm going to go."

"Berkeley is a five-hour drive from here!" Earl's voice trembled. "What are you going to do, live with Chic?"

"Yes."

Earl walked around the room shaking his head. "Not now, Beth. I need you now. Everything is falling apart. I've never asked for much. Not now, don't do this now!"

Beth exhibited her usual composure. "It's true you never asked for much, but you haven't given much, either. You never asked if I was happy or even satisfied. Since I've come back from my mother's, you haven't asked what happened or even how she is— how I am or if we talked. The big event for you was going to the mall by yourself and warming some frozen dinners."

Beth's voice was rising and her eyes flashed. She didn't display anger often and seeing it now frightened Earl.

"Stuff happened to me too, but you never cared enough to hear it. You haven't been there for me for a long time, and I don't feel like holding your hand through this. Grow up. Make your own decisions." Beth stood and walked out of the room, leaving Earl to stare at her acceptance letter in stunned silence.

He knew he needed to get away. He walked out the front door and just kept going. By the time he calmed enough to be aware of his surroundings, it was dark, and he was miles from home. Seeing a phone booth, he called Beth.

When she answered, her voice was soft, conciliatory. "Where are you?"

"Downtown—by the Taco Bell. Can you come get me?"

"Yes," she said. "I'm sorry. I'm so sorry. I didn't mean…"

"I know," Earl said. "We'll talk about it when you get here."

She picked him up, and they went back to their house and talked through the night. By morning they realized how long it had been since they had said anything real to each other. They made love, then talked some more. Exhaustion finally stopped their conversation.

Late in the next afternoon, they went out for breakfast. They were like they had been in the beginning, when they'd first met, both on the brink of change with decisions and choices to make. They fell in love anew and talked and hugged and comforted each other. It was as if they were twenty-two again.

A few days later, they went to their mountain cottage. After three weeks, Earl returned to town to formally quit. At the end of the summer, Beth left for Berkeley, where she would share an apartment with Chic and start her new life. They rented out their house, and Earl settled into their vacation cottage to begin the singular process of finding his future.

Maria's Second Step

The elegantly attired banker, Hinckley Harper, approached the order counter of Mike's Magic Burgers with his hand extended. "Mike, nice to see you."

The approach was incongruous for someone walking into a burger joint, but no more so than the banker's two-thousand-dollar Armani suit. Mike smiled. "Mr. Harper, you have a very nice looking suits."

"Hinckley, please." He looked down at his suit, navy with the thinnest of red pinstripes. "Thank you. I have an uncle who's quite a Beau Brummell. We're the same size. I take his old stuff."

"Really!?"

"You don't think branch bankers make this kind of money, do you?"

Mike shrugged.

"The people who work in the corner branch aren't the 'highly paid bankers' you read about in the paper.

My uncle is a politician—that's where the money is. The senator receives a nice salary, does stock trading—that would be illegal for you and me but, somehow, isn't for him—and receives gifts and favors, which may technically be illegal, but, well, most of our politicians get rich on the job. Who's going to challenge him? He has a great life. I'm lucky to be the same size as he is."

"Senator?" Earl said.

"Yes. Senator Hinckley. My mother gave me her maiden name as a first name. Because of it, the senator has always had a soft spot for me. He tells everyone I was named for him."

Maria's arrival interrupted the men. Her dated, hippie clothing had been replaced by a soft jersey knit wrap dress in a small-flower pattern and low-heeled pumps. Her long hair was bound in a loose bun.

Mike spoke first. "Maria, you look wonderful. Turn around, let me see. It's perfect!"

Maria smiled. "I feel a little silly. Is it really okay?"

Mike stepped out from behind the counter to hug her. "Yes, it's really nice. You look beautiful."

She fussed with her hair when they separated.

Hinckley stepped forward. "Ms. Smithe, you look lovely. Not that you didn't always look fine, of course, or that I mean anything fresh—you know."

Maria gave a satisfied smile. "Thank you, Hinckley. Let's sit. I want to brief you before the others get here."

She began as soon as they were seated. "It has been a remarkable few months. The expansion of the store was a resounding success. By Thanksgiving it was clear that holiday sales would exceed my most extravagant hopes. One of the investors I'd been talking with stepped forward with enough money to open five more Animal World stores. If successful, there will be a small stock offering to expand throughout the region and then a larger public offering to take us national.

"Today you will meet three people I've hired to help with the expansion," Maria said. "They have extensive retail experience."

"Do they know about the burgers?" Hinckley asked.

Maria snickered. "I did my hiring interviews here. Ask me about that sometime. So, yes, they know."

As if on cue, two women and a man walked into the restaurant. Each wore a navy- blue suit with a white shirt and carried a soft leather briefcase. Maria raised her hand to attract their attention. With the similarity of their dress and movement they looked like a marching band coming across the restaurant. Maria introduced them.

"This is Chandra Lorain. She comes to us from the Gap and is our vice president, marketing." The blue suit with the soft paisley scarf, navy stockings, and high heels stepped forward, hand extended.

"E. Tyler Jackson comes to us from Starbucks and is now vice president, finance. The blue suit with pants and a patterned yellow tie, stepped forward, and extended his hand.

"Kimberlee Dellecourt is from Neiman Marcus and is now our vice president, operations." The blue suit with a European striped tie, taupe stockings, and medium heels extended her hand.

Mike approached their table expertly carrying the

five plates. "Finance?" he said. Tyler raised his hand.

"Marketing?" Chandra raised her hand.

To Kimberlee, he said, "You must be Operations."

And to Hinckley and Maria, he said, "And you get Basic Business Burgers. Enjoy."

They took their first bites in unison. No time was wasted on pleasantries. Chandra spoke about the creation of a logo, general site selection, marketing strategies, and the public relations campaign that would include appearances by Maria.

Tyler explained how the whole business would pay for itself and generate enormous profits.

Kimberlee described staffing, equipment needs, and specific site requirements. When finished, she handed Hinckley a binder that contained write-ups of what each of them had said and supporting documents.

Mike was at the table when they finished. "Productive meeting?"

"Yes," the three executives said in concert. Then they stood, shook hands with Hinckley, Mike, and Phil Reardon, who happened to be walking by. "See you back at the office," they said to Maria, and marched out.

Hinckley looked stunned. "I'm not sure I could have kept up with them if I hadn't eaten the burger."

"Awesome, aren't they?" Maria said.

"How much do people like that cost?" Hinckley asked.

"Not nearly as much as you'd think," Maria said. "We're giving them stock. They're betting on the come."

"But how did you talk them into selling…"

Maria finished his sentence, "…junk?"

"Yeah."

"Aside from Chandra, I'm not sure they know what we sell," Maria said. "It doesn't seem to matter."

Earl Meets Destiny

Earl spent over two months at the second home, that he and Beth called their "mountain cottage." Though the name suggests a remote and rustic setting, the area was best known for the charming downtown with its high-end boutiques, jewelry stores, art galleries, gourmet restaurants, wine tastings, and the many celebrities who frequented it.

Even though Earl had suffered no hardship, he was happy to be back in town and delighted to see Dee come forward to greet him when he walked into Mike's Magic Burgers.

"Earl, you look great!" she said, giving him a sincere and vigorous hug. "Time in the mountains has been good for you."

There had been no one near the cottage who would just listen to him. As the two settled into a quiet corner booth, Earl was thrilled at the opportunity to tell his story.

"After Beth left for school, I changed my life. I meditated, did yoga, and read, and read, and read—just about anything I could get my hands on. For the first time in years I had new ideas every day, new insights. It was wonderful. Then one morning, the amount of sugar I had just filled the bowl and that seemed like a sign to me. I knew, just knew, that I was ready for something to happen. That I would not need to buy a bag of sugar."

Earl laughed. "That sounds crazy doesn't it?"

Dee nodded. "A little, but I know what you mean."

"During my meditation I told the universe I was ready for something to come along. That afternoon, my neighbor, Les Goodman—he's principal at the high school—came over and started telling me about a career-education program he wanted to start. He got the funding, but only had a very small window of time for filling the position—if he failed then he'd lose the money. He said he'd like to hire someone from outside academia.

"It sounded like something I could do. So I asked if he'd consider me. He said I was just the sort of person he'd hoped to find. I'm going in for interviews next week. If they approve his recommendation, I'll take the job and move into town."

"I have a small guesthouse you could use," Dee said. "Whoever moves in will have to help with the garden, take care of the chickens, and generally help with maintenance and upkeep. The woman who was living there just moved a couple of days ago. Her work hours increased, and she didn't have time to enjoy the setting or help with the work."

"You have chickens?" Earl asked.

"Actually the chickens belonged to the woman who's moving. She's leaving them," Dee said.

"Are you allowed to have chickens in town?" Earl asked.

"Yes," she said. "Many enlightened communities allow small backyard flocks. Anyway, you'll need to see the place. Then you can tell me if you're interested."

A tall woman pulled a wheeled suitcase into the restaurant, made a quick survey of the room, then walked to the table where Earl and Dee sat and waited for Dee to acknowledge her.

Dee, involved in her conversation with Earl, had not seen her come in and did not immediately notice her standing next to the table. When she did, she stood and took the woman into her arms. "Dee Dee, what a surprise! Why didn't you let me know you were coming? Not that it matters. I'm so glad you're here."

"Mom, it's nice to see you too. You will not believe what happened. I was on my way to LA, but my flight was forced to land in Monterey because of a mechanical problem. The airline doesn't usually fly out of there, so they put us on a bus for San Jose which had a flight with plenty of room. A tanker turned over on the freeway, and we were detoured through town. Then the bus broke down two blocks from here.

"I called my agent to let her know I'd be late. She

said not to worry—there'd been some small catastrophe at each of the stores where I was scheduled to speak this week. I figured it must be fate that I spend the time here."

Earl stared at the tall woman.

"Earl, this is my daughter, Dee Dee."

He stood and put his hand out. "Destiny. Destiny Robertson. I saw you play against the Lady Vols."

Dee Dee took his hand, "That was a long time ago. Not many people recognize me anymore."

"That was the best basketball game I ever saw. I could have sworn you stuffed it. I was surprised the newspaper didn't talk about it."

"There were a few of us who swore I stuffed it, but people weren't ready to see a woman do that." She smiled and looked down at Earl's hand, still vigorously pumping her own.

"Sorry," Earl said, letting go of her hand, but continuing to stare. "You were great. You look the same. You're still…"

"Earl," Dee said. "It's rude to stare! Where are your manners?"

"I'm sorry." Earl turned to Dee and smiled. "It's just that you've been telling me that destiny was trying to get my attention, and I didn't believe you. I didn't believe destiny was looking for me. Now, here she is. Destiny's found me."

"Earl," Destiny said, "I assure you, I have not been looking for you. Right now I'm having enough trouble finding myself."

Fishy Burger

It no longer bothered Daphne to wait at the order counter of Mike's Magic Burgers—she knew the food would be terrific. While there, she exchanged acknowledgments with people she recognized from previous visits, noted that her favorite booth was empty, and generally felt content with the realization that she considered herself a regular.

She'd tried to explain Mike's to a friend. "If it's so wonderful, why don't you go there every day—twice?" he'd asked. It was a good question. Why didn't she? She'd told him she thought of a meal at Mike's as a brief vacation, a getaway. The answer did not satisfy her friend.

Mike walked out of the kitchen drying his hands on a towel and shamelessly brandishing his dimples. "Sorry to keep you waiting. Special Burger?"

Daphne took a moment to admire him, and said, "Not today. What's the Fishy Burger like?"

"The Tropical Burger with fins."

"Sounds perfect."

As usual, Daphne had barely settled into her booth when Mike slid the plate in front of her. She'd started to look forward to him saying "Enjoy."

"Thanks," she said, then lifted the burger with both hands and took a small bite to see what it tasted like. Delicious, of course. Then she closed her eyes and took a larger bite to see where it took her.

Opening her eyes, she discovered she was under-water, beside a rusted, glacier-blue, '55 Chevy, parked in a seaweed forest. Fish of various sizes and colors were swimming in small groups around her. She wanted to join them. Looking down at herself, she saw this burger gave her a fish-size, mermaid body. Thrilled, she tried to move—only to discovered that having a mermaid body did not mean she knew how to use it.

While she struggled to get the hang of mermaid propulsion, most of the fish gave her wide berth. In her ineptness, she ran into a fish only slightly smaller than she was. He turned menacingly, and hung in front of her, face-to-face, staring at her.

She apologized, explaining that she was usually a human, her tail wasn't the same as legs, and that she really wasn't a good swimmer as a person, either. She became concerned when a second fish appeared, and the two seemed to be commiserating. Appearing to end their conversation, one moved to each side of her—they were going to help her. They nudged her forward with their fins and by curling their tails around behind her. As they swam, she experimented with various movements in order to figure out what worked. When she went off course, one or the other of the fish would nudge her back in line.

Curious, she steered them into the car. Looking around, she remembered the last time she was in the back seat of a '55 Chevy and felt herself blush. She and her companions swam around to the trunk, and Daphne laughed. Next to the spare tire was a neatly folded blanket with two unopened quarts of beer on top of it.

She'd gotten the hang of swimming like a mermaid. So she thanked the fish as best she could and went off to explore on her own.

Moving into the seaweed forest, she joined a group of yellow striped fish that swam back and forth. The maneuver took a great deal of her still developing skills to accomplish. Once she had, she wondered why they were doing it and looked for a different group to join.

The orange fish swam very fast then stopped suddenly, stayed still for long moments, then rushed forward again. As with the first group, the movements were initially challenging, but quickly became boring. She wondered what the fish were intending to do by swimming like this.

She joined some blue-green fish that, though in a group, did not swim in unison. She followed a bunch of them to the engine compartment and in and around the deteriorating remnants of the various mechanisms. Their movements were less rigorous than the other groups, but more challenging because they changed all the time.

Seeking out nooks and crannies, they seemed to invent games, sometimes swimming gracefully, other times ramming one another aggressively. They seemed to just want to have fun and that worked for her.

Feeling exhilarated, she swam into an open space and performed a ballet meant to express her joy at being there and meeting all the fish. A few of them joined her, adding to the drama; others sent encouragement in their own ways.

Without thinking, she closed her eyes and was back at the restaurant with Mike sitting across the table smiling at her. "You look happy."

She giggled. "I love those little fishes kissing me all over."

Earl's New Job

After months without a schedule, Earl's first week back in town seemed hectic to him. Monday, Tuesday, and Wednesday mornings, he underwent interviews to determine his suitability to run the high-school level career-counseling class.

Fortunately, Les had warned him about the process. "Be bland but attentive, slightly deferential but not so much you look weak," he'd said. "Everyone you'll talk with attended the same interview training, so the questions are likely to be, more or less, the same each day, but don't mention the sameness. Nothing upsets them more then being told they are not being original."

Indeed, the same questions were asked at all the meetings, and by Wednesday Earl felt he had a better understanding of brainwashing techniques.

Optimistic about his chances of getting the job, he spent his afternoons painting Dee's guesthouse and learning how to take care of the chickens, the garden, and the small greenhouse. He was surprised by the volume of food produced in the compact space and how little work was required.

Later each afternoon, he and Destiny went to the park and played basketball. It was obvious Earl was the weaker player and they spent most of their time improving his game.

Thursday Les called Earl to tell him he had the job. He went to the school that afternoon to sign papers. "It's so good to have you on board," Les said. "Glad you made it through the gauntlet."

"I doubt I would have if you hadn't warned me," Earl said. "They all asked the same questions."

"I know," the principal said.

"If they're all going to ask the same questions, why not just have one interview?"

Les smiled. "They represent different constituents. The theory is that the separate interviews give each group a chance to address their particular concerns.

"Monday you met with the faculty group. They were primarily concerned about your qualifications. They were not happy that you hadn't worked in education, but they know that if we don't fill the position, we lose the funding. If they'd been given time to argue, or it had been a full-time job, they would not have been this lenient.

"Tuesday you met with the parents group, a requirement imposed by the local PTA. Since very few parents are home weekdays, we draw from a very limited pool.

"Wednesday you met with the diversity group. They had to be sure you aren't prejudiced against anyone or anything."

"No one asked me about diversity issues," Earl said.

"To ask would itself be discriminatory, so they can't," Les said.

"How can they tell if I have prejudices?" Earl asked.

Les indicated with a gesture and a look that he had no idea. "Everyone wants to participate, but no one wants to accept responsibility, so they usually go along with what's suggested, especially if it's been suggested by me. A big incentive for them is that I like to put my opponents in charge of solving problems." Les laughed. "It's a system that has proven successful in getting buy-in.

"Don't get the wrong idea. You're part-time. If you do well and we get full-time funding, you'll be fired so a real academic can be brought in. You're fine for the experiment."

"But expendable?" Earl said.

"Exactly. We have the funding for one semester. I was given private assurance of a second semester—but no one should know that. If they thought we had two semesters, they'd have insisted on hiring an academic."

"Gotcha," Earl said.

"I've arranged for you to have an office. It's a converted storage closet under the stairs, no window, and quite small. Not what you're used to, I know, but it's considered an honor, so don't complain openly."

Les handed Earl a two-inch stack of papers. "This is some information you'll need; there's a handbook, parking information, and school rules; three forms to complete if you want insurance, four if you don't; several interesting articles, recent legal decisions regarding teachers, and a list of indications the kids have gotten to you and you need counseling."

Earl inhaled audibly.

"Just look through it. You're going to do fine. Likely this will be easier and more rewarding than any other work you've ever done.

"I don't expect you to be an academic; I have plenty of them. I hope you'll give the kids a different focus. The better I think you are, the less comfortable the rest of the faculty will be with you—so don't expect public praise from me. When dealing with the other teachers, bear in mind that many of them are about the same age emotionally as their students. I'd guess it won't take you long to figure out who the three or four adults on the faculty are.

"Tommy Thomson will stop by your office in a day or so. He and a couple of friends want to videotape part of your class for extra credit in art. I think it could work out, but I told him he'd need to talk with you. They're nice kids, no trouble. Think about how it could work for you.

"Scott Pulchanka will ask you to help with after-school activities. He always needs people to coach. He'll probably try to get you to work with the fuck-ups. Mostly they're kids from lousy homes. You could do them a lot of good, but they can be tough to deal with—you can take it; you're fresh."

Les reached behind him and presented a strip of cardboard with Earl's name neatly lettered on it. "This is for your door, temps don't get printed ones.

"My door is always open to you. Most of the teachers arrive and leave on schedule. So early morning and late afternoon there will be no one here to see you in my office and claim preferential treatment." Les held out his hand to Earl, indicating that the conversation was ended.

Earl's head whirled as he walked to his new home in Dee's guesthouse. He opened the note taped to his door and smiled when he saw it was from Destiny. She told him that it was nice to meet him and that she was happy he would be there for Dee. She thanked him for offering to handle her mail and said she'd be back soon. She told him he should keep playing basketball—that he had talent.

He was proud that he'd played ball with Destiny.

Tofu Burger

Mike was in the restaurant kitchen making some Decision Sauce, when he heard a conversation coming from the direction of the order counter. "Be there in a second," he shouted. A few minutes later, he went to the counter, expecting to find at least two people waiting, but only a skinny young man, with a prominent Adam's apple, stood there. He had a shadow of black hair on his head and a tiny blue-black goatee. His body swayed, and his limbs moved randomly, while he spoke to someone only he could see, whom he called Lyndon. In the conversation, the young man questioned the legitimacy of some thirteen votes.

Seeming to sense Mike's presence, he stopped mid-sentence, and turned. "Hey, man, you been there long?"

"Just a few seconds," Mike said.

"Shoulda said somethin'," the boy said.

"Didn't want to interrupt."

"Oh yeah, that's thoughtful." The young man fidgeted, shifting his weight from side to side. His head nodded and turned, and his arms moved without discernible purpose. "Hey, dude, this is, like, a real old hippie place, cool. I'm, like, a vegetarian. You got a Tofu Burger?"

Mike pointed. "At the bottom of the menu."

"Yeah, but, like, what does it do?" the boy asked.

"What do you mean?" Mike asked.

"Like, all the others, take ya to a desert island, or somethin'," the boy said, waving toward the descriptions on the menu.

"It tastes good," Mike said.

"Yeah, but what about the magic?" the young man asked.

"It's tofu. There's nothing magic about tofu."

The young man swayed and twitched. "Yeah, well, I'm hungry. I'll try one."

No one had ordered one in a while, so Mike had to look up the recipe. Delivering the sandwich, he was as unobtrusive as possible, so as not to interrupt the conversation between the boy and invisible Lyndon, which by this time had progressed to questioning why Nixon's treasonous interference in the peace negotiations with Vietnam weren't made public.

"Hey, dude, thanks," the young man said to Mike, quickly returning to his other conversation.

Mike went back to the counter and watched, not because he was expecting magic, but because he wanted to be sure the odd young man was all right. The youngster took a small cautious bite, then closed his eyes and took a large one. All the movement in his body stopped. He looked quiet and content. He ate slowly. When finished, he wiped the corners of his mouth and sat completely still, looking satisfied—happy. It looked like magic. Mike had never seen this with the tofu burger.

On his way out, the young man stopped and leaned across the counter toward Mike, and winked. "No magic, uh? That was great, dude. You'll be seein' me again."

"Hey," Mike said. "When you came in, were you talking with Lyndon Johnson?"

"Yeah. He wants me to write about him. How did you know who it was? I thought only I could see or hear him."

"I know a little of his story…heard some of what you said."

"Yeah. He's dead, you know. But still an interesting guy."

Mike watched the youngster leave, his nervousness and movements gone, his conversation with the spectral remains of Lyndon Johnson ended. It looked like magic. But it was a Tofu Burger, and everyone knows there's nothing magic about tofu.

Earl in the Classroom

Earl stood at the front of his class on the first day of the winter term. After taking attendance and making basic introductions, Earl handed out the papers he'd brought with him. He'd been careful to keep his instructions clear, just like one of the articles Les had given to him recommended.

"Okay, here's a course outline," he said. "We are going to meet with people in the community in order to find out what it's like to do their job."

He was relieved that the kids quieted down when he started talking. He'd been afraid they wouldn't. He felt more confident as he went on.

"You are going to look at the list of people available to be interviewed and decide who you would most like to talk with and who you would like to talk with second most. You will be working in teams of three to five people. The interviews will be taped. Each group will prepare a presentation for the rest of the class using the tape and other information you think is relevant. After all the presentations have been made, the interviewees will come to a pizza party, so we can thank them, and everyone can meet everyone else.

"Questions?" Earl pointed to a young man in the back of the room.

"What if we don't know what we want to be?" he asked.

"Pick the one that sounds the most interesting," said Earl.

"What if none of them sound interesting?" another student asked.

"Pick the one that sounds the least objectionable," Earl said.

"What if you're rich and don't need to work?" a third student asked.

"Go see the artist. Art offers many job opportunities if you don't need money," Earl said.

"What are we going to ask these people in the interview?" asked a girl sitting in the front row.

"I'll give you a list of standard questions, so the groups can compare the answers from different respondents. Each group will also come up with its own questions—basically, what do you want to know? We'll discuss etiquette before you conduct the interviews," Earl said.

Earl let them out of class early. He remembered his teachers doing that the first day of a class.

The selection process went smoothly—everyone got his or her first choice. Less than two weeks later, Earl was monitoring discussions by the first two groups to complete their interviews about what sort of presentation they would make to the others. They were working at opposite sides of a large room, but by the end of class, the groups were restless and started talking loudly across the room to one another.

"Mr. Witherspoon, what are we supposed to cover in these presentations?" a skinny boy asked in a squeaky voice.

"Whatever you believe the rest of the class would find interesting," Earl said. "Remember, you have the video. Think about how you want to use it. The art students will do the editing."

"Yeah, but, like, is this just about work stuff, or is personal stuff important too?" the skinny boy persisted.

A girl piped in. "Yeah, I think it's really cool that Steve the garage guy takes his wife to New York every year so they can go to the theater and opera."

"That's stupid stuff. Who wants to know that?" a young man replied.

A few "yeahs" were heard from around the room.

The same girl responded, "It may not make any difference to you, but girls want to know what kind of guy they're marrying. Even with all the woman's lib stuff, a woman can still be stuck with her husband's life."

"Where do you get this stuff, Julie?" another girl asked. "And what's so great about the opera anyway?"

"Yeah, why do you want to listen to a bunch of people screaming," one boy asked—others laughed.

Julie looked at the other girl. "You get to dress up."

The other girl's face changed. "How do you know?"

"My mom took me," Julie said.

"And you wore a fancy dress?"

Julie nodded. "With sequins on it. And I had my hair and makeup done."

"How do you know Steve's wife gets to dress that way?"

"She could, if she wanted to, and he'd wear a suit." Julie was now the center of attention.

"Ugh! Who cares about that?" the boys chorused.

"Yeah, how much money does he make?" someone said.

The girls sat quietly watching as the boys made their loud wisecracks. Earl allowed the revelry to continue a few seconds too long, during which the boys became self-conscious and then belligerent.

One turned to Julie. "Yeah, your mom and her highfalutin ideas are why your dad left her and married someone else."

"Billy!" Earl said.

"It's okay, Mr. Witherspoon." Julie calmly turned to the boy. "It sure is! And while my mom and I were in Hawaii last year, his new wife got to sit home and pop corn and watch old movies. They told me about it when we got back. Who do you think had more fun?"

There was a slight pause, then another youngster spoke up. "Our group interviewed Harvey. He's all about money."

"If he makes a lot of money, he must be a good therapist," another added.

"My dad says, 'He charges so much, you're crazy if you don't figure out how to get well fast,'" someone else said.

"Yeah, but he's kind of a jerk." The boy adopted a stance intended to represent the doctor. "He's all, 'And this is my leather couch. It costs three-thousand dollars. And this is my Porsche and my suits.'"

Another student added, "I think he's a jerk because he dates Dr. Phillips' receptionist, and she has small tits."

"Yeah, I'd date Dr. Forrest's receptionist."

"Wouldn't anyone?" another youngster opined.

"Anyone but a dork," a boy with complexion problems added.

"Okay, okay," Earl interrupted. "When you say the opera is stupid, or you prefer large-busted women, you are telling us about your preferences. Your job in this class is to tell us about other people. In your presentations, give the facts, and let the audience decide for themselves what they think."

"Yeah, but everyone likes big tits." There was a general laugh.

Earl faced the boy. "Do they?"

"Well sure …" the boy started, but then chose not to pursue the issue.

"Okay, now go home and think about what things each of you personally want to see in your group's presentation. When you meet again, remember: compromise is essential in teamwork. Keep in mind that each team will grade its own members for participation and cooperation, and those grades will be part of your overall grade for the class."

Two hours later, Earl sat at a large table in the center of Mike's Magic Burgers. Lips pursed, he threw envelopes into stacks, giving an exasperated "tsk" or "um" after each one.

Dee joined him, tea in one hand, scone in the other. "What's all this?"

"Destiny's mail. I didn't realize how much work it would be when I offered to sort through it and forward the important stuff."

Dee smiled. "Is this the first time you've done a favor for someone?"

Earl began to protest but then felt sheepish. "You know, I think it is. Not that I didn't mean to, but it always ended up being my secretary or my wife who did the work." The admission had made him feel mischievous. "You know, it was easier that way," he said.

"I bet it was." Dee picked up an old book from the table. Its cover was torn and mended. It bore the library identifier on its spine. "And this?"

"It's about raising chickens. The librarian gave it to me. She said no one's checked it out in ages."

"Are the chickens okay?"

"I don't really know. That's why I thought I'd read a little about them. Can we have chicks?"

"It's easier if one of the hens goes broody," Dee said. "Our birds are commercial crosses, and that's pretty much bred out of them."

"They don't sit on the eggs?"

"Not usually. There's an old brooder in the garage. It's fun to watch them hatch. Before you start, make sure you're up to it. You'll need to turn the eggs two or three times a day for twenty-one days. Then figure out what you're going to do with the birds. We don't have room for many more, and we only need one rooster. One of the neighbors used to kill birds for me, but he died, and it isn't easy to find someone with that skill."

"Kill birds?" Earl said.

"I never could do it," Dee said. "Even though those young, fresh chickens are delicious."

"I need to think this through," Earl said.

"How's your class going?" Dee asked.

"Different from what I expected." Earl frowned. "The kids are smarter than I thought—especially the girls."

"And the boys?"

Earl shook his head. "I can't see how they'll ever catch up. I see myself at that age, so immature and awkward. I wonder if I've caught up yet. I'm supposed to be teaching these kids, but it seems I'm the one learning."

"I'm sure they're learning too," Dee said.

"Yeah, but I don't know what they're learning," Earl said.

"No one ever does, for sure."

John's Decision

It was late afternoon when John walked into Mike's Magic Burgers dressed in his usual coveralls and wearing a serious look. "I'll have a Decision Burger," he told Mike, then seated himself in a quiet corner. As wearworn and self-absorbed as he was feeling, he remembered to say, "Thank you," when Mike slid the plate in front of him and said, "Enjoy." He took a deep breath before lifting the burger, closing his eyes, and taking a big bite.

When he opened his eyes he was standing in the hall of a government-type building, with shiny terrazzo floors. A woman with two pair of glasses, one she wore and the other she hung by a cord around her neck, sat at a metal desk.

John cleared his throat and waited for her to acknowledge him. She looked up from the book she was reading, took off the pair of glasses she had on, and lifted the pair that had been hanging on her chest onto her nose. "Can I help you?"

"I'm from Mike's, and I have a decision to make," John said and heard his voice waver.

"What kind of decision?" she asked.

"Career," John said.

She pointed. "Room D down the hall."

"What does D stand for?" John asked.

"Decision," the woman said.

"Are there other rooms?"

"No." The woman sounded concerned. "You want to make a decision, don't you?"

"Yes. But if there's only one room to go to, why do you need to be here?"

"So you go to the right place."

"But there's only one place."

"Yes, and lucky for you, it's the right one."

John swallowed the rest of his query, and said, "Thank you, ma'am."

"You're welcome, son." The woman smiled and nodded. "It's not often someone takes an interest in my work."

In Room D, John faced a disheveled man sitting behind a metal desk, very like the receptionist's. "Hello, son. What can I help you with?" he asked.

"I need to decide about a career," John said.

The man stood and then moved around the room. He touched the corner of each of the bookcases that lined one wall. John noticed the books all became job and career related. Returning to the seat behind his desk, he turned over the diploma hanging on the wall so it showed a career counseling credential. A copy of *What Color Is Your Parachute* appeared on the desk.

"There," the man said. "Now, let's start."

"I'm in college, studying to be an accountant," John said. "In the meantime, I'm working as an auto mechanic."

"That sounds admirable," the man said.

"I hate the accounting classes, but I love my job."

"Oh," the man said.

"I'm also not very good at accounting," John said, "but I'm an excellent mechanic."

"Uh huh," the man said.

"What should I do?"

"What do you want to do?" the man said.

"Stop studying business and start studying engineering—but not just the math and drawing—I still want to work with my hands," John said without hesitation.

"Why don't you?"

"Catherine."

"What about Catherine?" the man asked.

"I'm afraid she'll leave me. I'm afraid she wants to marry someone who does a fancy job and makes a ton of money," John said. "I could end up being a mechanic my whole life."

"Can you be happy as an accountant?"

"I don't see how," John said. "I don't like it. I'm not good at it. It's not what I want to do."

"Is there another profession that attracts you?"

"No. I like working with my hands. I'm good at figuring out mechanical stuff."

"Do you think you're pleasant company when you're unhappy?"

"No," John said.

"Do you think Catherine wants to be with someone who's miserable and unpleasant?"

"No," John said. "But what if she wants to marry a professional, someone who wears a suit and tie?"

"Have you asked her?"

"No."

"You should."

"I'm afraid," John said. "What if she leaves me?"

"Well, I guess you'll have to give up what you really want in order to make her happy." The man gave a quick confident nod.

John shook his head. "That doesn't sound like good advice."

"What do you think good advice would be?"

"Find someone who shares my views and accepts what I want," John said.

"Which is?"

"To be the best mechanic around. To invent things that make the world a better place."

"Any other questions?" the man said.

"No, sir, I guess not." John felt more resigned than satisfied when he returned to Mike's.

"Okay?" Mike said.

"Yeah, but why is that woman there directing people?" John said.

"So they go to the right place."

"But there's only one place to go."

"And it's the right one," Mike said.

Earl's Success

Earl's course was a hit. The people being interviewed enjoyed telling their stories. The kids loved having a chance to talk to adults about what they did. The art students did a great job editing the videos. The presentations were different from one another in style and content, and interesting to watch. They were so good they were put in the library, so all the students could see them. Even without a teaching credential, Earl had made a few friends among the faculty and was accepted into the general teacher population. No one objected when Les told them he had the funding for a second semester, and Earl would be staying. But he still felt ungrounded. The hand-lettered nameplate on his door annoyed him every time he saw it—it was a symbol of his discontent.

After school let out for the summer, he went to his mountain cottage for a vacation with his wife, Beth, and their daughters. Laura stayed only a couple of days.

Chic stayed longer. She and Earl took walks through the woods every morning and talked.

"Do you miss Mom?" Chic asked.

"Oh sure," Earl said.

"She misses you too. I don't know how you can just live apart," Chic said.

"What don't you understand?" Earl asked.

Well, Dad, I'm not a kid anymore. I know how men are." Chic paused. "Do you have a girlfriend?"

Earl felt like he had at school; these kids were too smart. "No. I haven't even considered it," he said. But he had. Not much, but sometimes he got lonely. "I'm very busy with my new work," he told his daughter. "Is your mother concerned?"

"Not that I can tell. That's what makes me crazy," Chic said. "How can the two of you do this? Don't you worry about your relationship?"

He worried about it all the time, but he didn't think he should tell her that. He put out his arm and pulled her to him. "Chic, you're so brave to ask."

She wiggled away and stood, feet firmly planted, hands on hips, looking at him.

Earl grimaced. "You want a real answer, don't you?"

"Yes," Chic said.

"Chic, I don't know what's going to happen," Earl said. "When I think about it, I get scared. Your mom wants…I'm afraid to push."

His honesty was rewarded. She let the conversation end.

He and Chic were arm in arm when they walked back to the house, where Beth was making sandwiches for lunch. Seeing them she smiled. In that moment, Earl felt loved and realized how much he missed his family life.

After Chic left, Earl decided to take the bull by the horns. "Beth, I think we should talk."

"Good idea," Beth said.

"You first," Earl said.

"No." Beth smiled. "You brought it up. You obviously have something specific on your mind. I don't—I was just agreeing. What were you thinking?"

"What's going to happen?" Earl asked.

"I'm going to finish school and get a teaching job," Beth said.

"With us," Earl pressed.

Beth's face revealed nothing to him. "I don't know," she said.

"Will you come home?" Earl asked.

Beth winced. "I want it to be different. I don't know how we do that."

"All I ever wanted was you, Beth," Earl said.

Her face softened. "That's a beautiful, romantic idea, but what does it mean? You wanted me for what? To do the laundry? To run a house? To laugh at your jokes?"

Earl feigned indignation. "There's nothing wrong with my jokes."

Beth answered in kind. "Are you kidding?"

"What do you mean? The mailman joke is a real gem. If you've forgotten, I can tell it again, right now."

Beth laughed. "No. Please. I remember it."

"How about the Christmas Angel joke? That's a good one."

"Earl, I love you." Beth put her arms around him.

"Oh, Beth, I love you too."

Later, they lay on the floor in front of the fireplace, feeling the last heat from the red embers. Earl was on his side. His hand supported his head, while he looked at Beth with a silly grin. "When are you coming home?"

"For now, Berkeley is my home," Beth said.

He wanted to look strong in spite of the sick flutter in his stomach.

She put her hand on his cheek. "Earl, I never loved you more than right now. I never appreciated your kindness, tenderness, and faithfulness more then right now. But, I can't go back to what we were, and I don't know if we know how to live a different life." Her eyes were filled with tears.

He took her in his arms. "We don't have to settle this right now." He kept holding her while her body shook with deep sobs. He wondered if she noticed he cried too, but didn't ask.

They were alone for another ten days and treated each other gently, tenderly, carefully, and very lovingly. The one topic Earl wanted to talk about was ignored by both of them.

The Boys from Metro

Hinckley Harper stood near the entrance and slowly scanned Mike's Magic Burgers. After two scans, he approached the order counter. "Maria here?"

"Haven't seen her," Mike said. Pointing at Hinckley's jacket, he added, "Another great suit."

"Here, feel." Hinckley extended his arm.

"Oh. That's nice. What is it?"

"Real good wool. I didn't even know it could feel like that. It's the latest from my uncle. Say, you and I are about the same size…want me to call you next time he's getting rid of stuff? He has all kinds of things, not just suits."

"I haven't worn hand-me-downs since I was a kid."

"It's weird at first, but you get used to it," Hinckley said.

"I didn't realize politicians made that much money."

Hinckley nodded. "You should see his houses and

cars. He's a real whiz at developing his own net worth—too bad he can't do more for the rest of us."

Maria's entrance drew their attention. She wore a fitted navy suit, which might have given her a military bearing except that its tight fit so exaggerated her already curvy figure, both men spontaneously assumed an expectant position, as if ready to cover her or catch a body part, in case a button popped. The stiletto heels she wore made her look unsteady and added to the unnaturalness of the look.

Hinckley's reaction was immediate, "Oh! Look at you. It's so different. I mean, it's nice, but so different."

"It seems extreme to me too," Maria said, shaking her head and responding to his tone more than his words. "We're going on the road for the initial public offering. Chandra suggested an image consultant, and *this* is what she came up with. I think, unless I intend to accessorize with a small whip, softer would be better."

"Or even a medium whip," Hinckley said. "It could carry a medium whip."

"A holster and bandolier might work," said Mike. "Silver. They'd have to be silver."

"Okay, guys, that's what I thought too," Maria said. She turned to Hinckley. "Let's eat."

"Basic Business Burger or Finance?" asked Mike.

Maria looked at Hinckley. "Basic okay with you?"

"Yeah. Tyler and I talked about most of the finance business yesterday."

After they seated themselves, Hinckley said, "You're right on schedule, Maria. You must be very proud."

"Ask me again at the end of the year. There are still

things to do," Maria said.

Mike appeared and placed a burger in front of each of them. "Enjoy."

Maria began to talk after her first bite. "Hinckley, I'm grateful for your help, but I need to tell you something. This public offering stuff is a big deal. We're beginning to hear from New York and Chicago banks. We've even talked with someone from Credit Suisse. So far we've only needed one bank. I'm not sure how much longer…"

"I can help you," Hinckley said. "You are hearing from other banks, and with your growth, you feel you need to consider them, but you think it would be disloyal to me."

"You know," Maria said, then sighed. "I told Tyler I wanted to be the one to talk with you."

Hinckley nodded. "Tyler didn't have to tell me—that's business."

"I appreciate everything you've done. But it's not just me anymore."

"Maria, I know, and I have something to tell you, as well. With this public offering, the company will be too large to be handled by a branch. I will be bringing a vice president from our metropolitan division to meet you and Tyler."

"So you won't be the bank person in charge of the Animal World account?"

"No," Hinckley said.

"So you help a company grow, and the bank takes the account away from you?" Maria asked.

"Yes," Hinckley said, nodding.

"Does that make you angry?"

Hinckley shook his head. "If I wanted to work with big companies, I could apply to the metro or the national divisions. I like working in the branch. It's what I want to do."

"So I needn't worry about talking with other banks?" Maria said.

"Not a bit. The boys from metro know what they're up against," Hinckley said. "And when the chain goes national, your account will be moved up to the national division. If you ever think they are not doing a good job for you, switch banks."

"I'm so grateful for your help."

"And I am delighted at your success."

They were both looking at their empty plates when Mike said, "Okay?"

They smiled at each other, then at Mike, and said, "Yes," at the same time and laughed. They hugged before parting at the door.

Earl Meets Mr. Grants

An ebullient Earl danced into Mike's Magic Burgers and went straight toward the table at back of the restaurant, where Dee sat behind the 'Palms Read $10' sign, reading a book. "Dee, I've got great news!" he shouted while still twelve feet away from her. "I'm going to make a PBS special!"

"How did that happen?" she asked, as he sat in the chair across the table from her.

"Les, the principal, he showed the videos from last semester to a professor up at the university. The guy really liked them and said he thought he might find a grant that would pay for us to go around the country doing similar ones."

She made a down motion with her hands. "Use your inside voice."

He looked around to see everyone looking at him. "Sorry. Sorry," he said to anyone whose eye he caught.

"And?" Dee said.

"And the guy found the money," Earl said, in his inside voice. "And Les arranged for that guy, Pete Gardiner—they call him Mr. Grants—to meet me. And he came to my broom closet at the high school, and invited me to lead the team around the country. There won't be any pay, but all expenses will be covered. The high school is willing to keep me on the payroll through production, because if the videos make it to TV, it will bring them prestige."

"Earl, this sounds almost too good. Are you certain it's real?"

"I thought the same thing, so I checked the guy out. It wasn't hard; everyone knew about him," Earl said. "Somehow he's always there when things happen. He's sort of a scoundrel, but he's terrific at getting grant money. His projects generally lead to other opportunities, so people like working for him. But he keeps most of the money for himself."

"It doesn't sound fair or ethical," Dee said. "Are you going to do it?"

"Wouldn't miss it for the world," Earl said. "Oh, after the school administration heard about the grant, they gave me a fan for my office at school."

Dee smiled. "It's nice to be acknowledged."

Last Request

The old woman stood firmly planted in front of the order counter at Mike's Magic Burgers. Head high. Feet apart. Hands on hips.

"Mike, I want two Special Burgers—to go."

"Capitola, you know that's against the rules," Mike said. "What's up?"

It looked as if Mike's question pushed the air out of her. Her body settled down onto itself, and she appeared to shrink. Her bottom lip trembled. "Owen has taken a turn," she said.

"Are you sure the burger won't hurt him?"

"The doctor said nothing can hurt him, or help him, anymore—he is close to the end." A tear rolled down her cheek.

"Oh, Capitola." Mike walked around the counter, hugged the woman, and led her to a chair. "Sit. I'll get you a little sherry." He brought her the small glass of amber liquid. "I have this in the kitchen, for cooking, you know."

Capitola looked relaxed by the time Mike returned and presented her with a white carryout sack.

"I hope you don't really cook with that sherry," she said. "It's far too good for that." Looking at the bag, she continued, "This is one of three things Owen hoped for."

"Oh, yeah, right," Mike said, reaching behind the counter. "Here's his Cuban cigar. A customer gave it to me yesterday, saying I'd know who to give it to."

Capitola's eyes welled with tears again. "Two out of three…"

She was interrupted by the door opening, and the entrance of a shapely blonde who was dressed decades out of date. The woman shook her head as if to clear it.

"Where am I? I was playing gin rummy with Peter, and winning for a change, and all of a sudden, I'm here." She had a breathy voice.

Seeing Mike, she smiled. "Oh, Mike, it's you. I should have known." Looking around the restaurant, she said, "Have you painted since the last time I was here? It looks brighter. I like it."

Capitola squealed. "Marilyn Monroe? How did you know?"

"Owen and I talked," Mike said to Capitola.

"Marilyn, this is Capitola. Her husband, Owen, always hoped to meet you. The doctors say he's likely to be going home soon. You may be showing him the way. There's a burger in the bag for you—assuming you can eat it."

"Sure can, that's one of our perks," she said. "If he's

not quite ready, I'll hang around. Maybe we'll come back for more—I love your burgers."

Life Evaluation Burger

Earl wandered around the mall, looking in the windows and stopping for a cookie and a cup of coffee. Then he took a walk in the park. When neither made him feel better, he went to Mike's Magic Burgers, hoping he'd find someone to talk with.

"Earl, you look pathetic," Mike said. "What's wrong?"

"I feel lost," Earl said.

"What do you mean?"

"I feel like I'm running in circles," Earl said. "Like a dog chasing its own tail."

Mike shrugged. "Everyone feels like that sometimes."

"I thought Beth would come home. The things I'm doing—like the trip—I thought she'd be impressed and want to come. I thought I could persuade her to come back. Give up her school stuff."

Mike listened.

"She told me she already signed up to do some student teaching. Why can't she put that off? This trip will be a lot of fun."

Mike nodded.

"She says she wants her own life. What does that even mean? She has a life. She's my wife. I've been patient about this, but I miss the part where I'm her husband. How could she rather teach than be with me?"

"You're scared and lonely," Mike said.

"I wouldn't say scared or lonely."

"I know. That's why I said it for you. I have a burger called a Life Evaluation Burger, and it sounds like you're in just the right mood for it."

Earl stared at Mike. "I come here with serious concerns about my life and you suggest a burger?"

"Uh, yeah," Mike said. "This is a burger joint. That's what I've got. Find a seat, I'll bring it out."

Earl was incredulous at the suggestion that a burger might help him feel better, but he did as he was told. As he sat down, Mike slid the burger in front of him. "Enjoy."

Earl lifted the sandwich with both hands and took a small bite. It was great! He closed his eyes and took a large bite. It felt like he was being thrown back against his seat and pulled up a steep hill—like on a roller coaster but faster.

Looking around, he realized he was traveling through his life. He saw himself as a baby, his mother in a cotton house dress, and his father in the tired work clothes he always wore.

He saw himself grow, enter school, be observed by his father, cared for by his mother, and teased by classmates. There they were: Billy, Hank, and Walt—whatever happened to them?

Soon he was in high school, and people praised his work and encouraged him to pursue a profession. Mr. Wilson. He owed a lot to Mr. Wilson. He was the one who had suggested law school.

And then he was in college and won some competitions, was voted into office, chosen to do, picked to be, and saw his name in print.

There's Beth. He knew the first time he saw her she was the girl he wanted. Then she agreed to marry him. He relived the same fear and joy he had at their actual wedding. There's their first apartment with that awful red linoleum!

Then he was an attorney working to establish himself. Often away from home—working late. Laura was born. His main memory of her early years was of her sleeping.

Earl saw the two funerals that marked his parents' deaths only months apart. He felt a tightness in his chest and didn't know if it was emotion or increasing pressure from his uphill climb.

His second daughter, Chic, was born and he saw her grow. He drove both girls to school. Laura sat quietly in the back seat while Chic was in front chattering. Chic was so different from Laura, so much easier to be around, to talk with.

Laura graduated from high school with honors, and he felt awkward and didn't know what to say. Beth's parents were so proud of their granddaughter.

Chic graduated and she and Beth moved to Berkeley. He saw the recent summer break when he held Beth, and they seemed close.

He felt his climb ending and then, still like a roller coaster, he was on the top. It's today. He sees Mike give him a burger, and now it feels like he's going downhill. Is this the future? He's in his office at school, talking with a young girl, and she says no one ever took her seriously before him, and he's proud of his work. He sees Beth in school and happy, and he feels sad and wishes she were with him. There's Destiny and they're playing basketball. He's very happy and he goes on a trip and sees a lot of people and realizes he's entering a whole new life. The action is speeding up, he feels a revelation and sees himself coming home with it, and it somehow gives him a purpose.

Things are speeding by. He and Destiny are talking. What's that look? Things move faster yet, he sees Beth walk into Mike's with a man he doesn't know. It's all mixed up…he and Beth…what's Destiny doing there? Everything's moving too fast to see. Then he's walking down a city street, carrying a briefcase—things are no longer whizzing past.

He sees Laura finish medical school, and he doesn't know what to say. And then Chic says she wants to be a lawyer just like him, and he's proud.

Laura gets married, and Earl stands on the sidelines until Chic drags him into the pictures.

Chic gets married in a big church and then is holding a baby in her arms. Then Laura walks in, holding her own baby. And Earl is happy but doesn't know what to say.

Things are moving slower now. He sees himself get older, and he has grandchildren around him, and he smiles. He keeps getting older, it feels as if the ride is stopping, and then there is darkness.

When he opens his eyes he is looking at his empty plate. He hears Mike say softly. "What's the thing you most want to do?"

"Contact Laura," Earl said. "There's something else. Wait, I'm losing it. How do I keep it? I'm losing it."

"That's how it works. It's like a dream. Remember to contact Laura—that's the most important thing right now," Mike said. "You may think of other things during the next few days."

Earl called Laura as soon as he got home, but she didn't answer. He knew a phone message was inadequate for the task and decided to write a letter while he still had the strength of his convictions. In it he told her that he'd always felt awkward around her but that he loved her and wished they could be closer. He said he was very proud of her. He told her he could be a funny guy and asked her to give him a chance to be a better father. After he finished, he sealed the envelope and walked to the post office to mail it immediately, afraid he would lose his nerve.

Friends

Maria, dressed in one of her old gauze skirts and well-worn Birkenstocks, carried a cloth bag with green leaves sticking out the top, slung over her shoulder. Entering Mike's Magic Burgers, she sang out, "Delivery! Fresh eggs, fresh herbs!"

Mike came out of the kitchen wiping his hands on a towel. "Maria, why are you making the delivery?"

"I took a day off work and went to have coffee with Dee," Maria said. "She asked if I would do it."

"Why did you take the day off?" Mike asked.

"I'm a little blue," Maria said. "I need a day away from those corporate types. I'm delighted to see my vision for Animal World validated, and I like the money. But there are things about my old life that I miss, like coffee with Dee."

"Do you think you're blue because your original store was relocated to the mall?" Mike said.

"Maybe," Maria said. "I hope the store closing didn't hurt your business."

"Not at all!" Mike said. "The clientele changed after the store became Animal World. Magic wasn't a big seller to the mainstream-moms with their vans full of kids who shopped there. To be honest, they were making some of my customers a little nervous. I'm glad they're gone."

"They dropped the name Chicken Shit," Maria said.

"Too risqué for the kiddies?"

Maria nodded.

"You had to see that coming."

Maria shrugged. "I thought if I was successful I could break some rules, but it seems the more successful I am, the more strictly I'm held to them. It isn't as much fun as I'd hoped."

"Want a burger?" Mike asked.

Maria smiled. "Nah, just need to see friends. Be somewhere I can feel grounded and be myself. Sort out how I'm doing."

Mike put his arm around her. "I think you're doing great! If you want, you can help me. You can set up for lunch and then bus tables. That should help you put things in perspective."

"I'd like that," Maria said.

Hours later she wiped the last of the tables. "My feet hurt," she told Mike. "But I liked it. Thanks."

"Anytime," Mike said. "There's always something to do in a restaurant."

Destiny Comes Home

Having driven around in circles for almost thirty minutes, looking for the address where he was supposed to pick up Destiny, Earl was annoyed. She was returning from her trip. This was the last appearance. It was only thirty miles from home. He'd left in plenty of time and arrived as expected. But he could not find the address. He'd wanted to impress Destiny, show her that he could be cool, and now he was late. Finally, he decided to park and search on foot, only to realize he was directly across the street from his destination.

He entered through a flat wooden door that appeared to have been painted forest green but was now faded to a lighter shade, with Floyd's Books stenciled on it in silver, and was surprised to find himself in a spacious, well-lit, well-stocked bookstore. There were both new and used books, large sections of old and contemporary literature, aisle-end displays for small-press publications, and a collectors' section with first editions. He loved the way it smelled.

In the center of the space, a group of sixty or so, mostly women, sat on folding chairs, listening to Destiny. By the time he made his entrance, she had finished her presentation and was answering questions. He stood in the back of the room.

"Any more questions?" Destiny asked.

A woman in the middle of the audience raised her hand and then asked, "What is the hardest thing you have to do as part of your work?"

"The hardest thing for me is to stay on purpose," Destiny said. "If I worked for someone, they would assign me a persona, like a uniform, a badge, that could serve as armor. Since I am out in the world by—and as—myself, I don't have that armor to hide behind. For me, work and life are the same thing. I still have to protect myself from things that would distract and maybe hurt me. The hard part is to do that without cutting myself off from the world. The difference between distractions and opportunities, good advice and bad, isn't always obvious—they can look the same."

Destiny took a breath.

"My grandmother had a saying, which my mother hates, but sums it up for me: 'It's a great life, if you don't weaken.' I hope it means something to you."

The woman obviously in charge walked toward Destiny, applauding and saying, "Thank you, Ms. Robertson. That was lovely." To the crowd she said, "Ms. Robertson will be available at the side of the store to sign copies of her books."

Earl waited until most of the women had gone, before he approached her. "Destiny, I'm here. Sorry I was late."

Destiny's face lit with recognition. "Earl, look at you! You've changed. I hardly recognize you."

"Well, yes, I believe I have changed. But I didn't think I looked different," he said, with what he hoped looked like a bon vivant shake of his head. He'd always thought it was the jeans that made Mike look cool, and this confirmed it. He'd worn jeans and even though he was late, Destiny had noticed.

"I can look hip too," he thought. "It just takes some jeans and a plaid shirt. They'll be even cooler after they're washed."

Are They Legal?

Entering Mike's Magic Burgers, Daphne was surprised to hear angry shouts. She stood off to the side of the entrance—out of the way. Hearing this sort of anger in Mike's was out of character, like hearing cursing in church.

"Magic, schmagic," the police chief, recognizable by his uniform, yelled at Mike. "You and I both know what's going on here, and one of these days I'll prove it." He brushed against Daphne on his way out. "Magic sauce, my ass. Tastes like Thousand Island dressing to me," he said to the world at large.

Daphne stood plastered against the wall as the door closed behind the officer, and the patrons in the restaurant broke into enthusiastic applause.

From his place behind the order counter, Mike motioned for her to come in.

"What was that about?" she asked, walking toward

him.

"Old stuff. There was an incident, and Chet, the chief, always thought it was my fault," Mike said. "Lately he's been accusing me of using illegal drugs in my sauces."

"What sort of incident?" Daphne asked.

"His grandfather died at a wedding I catered," Mike said.

"Died?!" Daphne said, in a shrill voice.

"Sorry, sorry, it's not the way it sounds," Mike said. "Before there was a restaurant, a few of us started the business by cooking for friends. The Special Burger was our first commercial success. A couple was getting married in the park and asked us to cater the wedding. The sauce opens your heart to the love of the universe, so you see the goodness, beauty, and potential in yourself and those around you—it was the sixties; the burger fit right in. The day of the wedding was warm and sunny. People were feeling good. Adding the love of the universe would have been enough, but the Special Sauce got left out in the sun and became more potent. The group was libidinous to start, and then huge portions of the extra-strong sauce were dished onto the burgers. You can imagine what happened."

Daphne listened with rapt attention.

"The chief's grandfather had been very ill and confined for several months. The old man had insisted on attending this wedding. He ate a Special Burger, and then died in the arms of a twenty-year-old woman, with whom he had shared warm feelings. There was nothing untoward. The young woman said that during the brief time they were together, all they did was talk, but they felt an uncommon closeness and formed a bond."

Mike shook his head and took a deep breath.

"There was an investigation. The old man's doctor testified that he could have gone any time without provocation. Chet's grandmother was on our side. She said she was delighted that he felt that way at the time of his death and said he hadn't looked that happy in years. The young girl said he reminded her of her grandfather, and she was honored to have been able to see him into the next life. Her parents said she was like that. But Chet would hear none of it and blamed me for the death. Because of his efforts, I agreed not to serve Special Burgers."

"That's why they're not on the menu," Daphne said.

Mike nodded. "He knows I still serve them and periodically comes in and checks the kitchen for Special Sauce and what he calls 'other illegal drugs.' He never could tell one sauce from another so, as long as I don't label it Special Sauce I can leave it out."

"And you serve him Thousand Island dressing?"

"No," Mike said. "I serve him whatever he orders. Okay, *once or twice* I slipped him a Special Burger, just to see what would happen. He didn't notice a thing. He doesn't feel the magic—a lot of people never do."

"And the drugs?" Daphne said.

"If you're asking whether the sauces contain illegal drugs, the answer is not within the normal definition," Mike said. "Come into the kitchen."

Daphne was surprised to see potted plants. Some hung in front of the window; others were on a shelf under the bluish glow of florescent grow lights.

Mike stood like a professor, his arm gesturing toward the plants. "We'll start with the herbs. I use only fresh. Some of them, though legal, are hard to find in a store. I grow some here; others I buy from friends. All are grown using biodynamic principles. None are inspected or approved by any government agency. So are they legal? Technically, maybe not."

He opened a large cooler and pulled out a cupped tray of eggs. "I use only fertilized eggs from free-range chickens. I get these from a friend who has a flock in her backyard. So, again, legal?"

"But isn't that a health risk?" Daphne asked.

Mike shrugged. "Never had a lick of trouble."

Returning the eggs to the cooler, he removed a container of milk. "I use raw milk from cows that walk around a field and eat grass and are milked twice a day by a farmer who warms his hands before touching their udders."

Mike smiled, and his tone changed. "The farmer is such a sweet man," he said.

Returning to his professorial stance, he continued. "The milk is tested. The farmer's family drinks it. But it is not certified for sale. So, legal? Not really—but this is not the sort of illegal drug the chief is worried about."

Putting the milk away, Mike took out a box of hamburger patties. "I use beef from free-range cows certified organic and breads from a local bakery equally concerned about its ingredients."

"What about the magic? What makes the magic?" Daphne asked.

"Mike's has been in operation long enough that the restaurant itself has a certain energy," Mike said, "like a shrine or a church. But basically, real food is magic."

"That's it?"

"That's my part. You know, magic is magic. It goes where it wants."

"Are you afraid it will go away?"

"I treat it with respect and gratitude," Mike said. "That's all I can do."

"Are there magic addicts?"

"Occasionally someone starts eating here all the time, but if you overdo it, the magic stops working. Then they stop coming."

"So, magic?"

"Magic."

One on One with Destiny

Earl and Destiny were talking while casually shooting baskets at the local park. "Earl, you've been practicing!" Destiny said, leaning forward, hands on knees.

"Yup," Earl said. "How long has it been since you lived here? Does it still seem special to you, or is it just another place?"

Destiny took the ball and shot an easy layup. "I left over thirty years ago. Oddly, it still feels like home."

Earl retrieved the ball and was going for an easy one, when Destiny stole it and sank a shot herself.

"Next time try this." She took the position he held, showed him a defensive move then handed the ball to him, and they replayed it. This time he kept the ball and made the basket. "Again," she said, throwing the ball back to him. "Keep your knees soft. Better!" She grabbed the ball and threw it back to Earl. "Again. Yeah, now you've got it." She caught the ball as it fell and threw it to Earl. "One more time," she said. He made the shot. "Great."

"Ever think of coaching?" Earl asked.

"I'm old for it," Destiny said. "And the game's changed."

"Hey, you were the best! You've still got moves."

Destiny jumped up, intercepting what would have been Earl's first three-pointer of the day, landed, dribbled once, took a step, pivoted, and jumped, sinking her own shot. "Yeah, maybe I could coach," she said.

"Why did you come back?" Earl asked.

She stood, arm around the ball, hand on hip looking at him. "It just seemed like the thing to do." She dribbled and ran straight toward him, feinting right and then left around him to the bucket. "Ooooh, that one felt nice."

"Looked pretty too," Earl said.

"Thanks." She dribbled around the court then passed the ball. "What about you? Miss being a lawyer?"

He laughed and shook his head. Holding the ball in front of him, he swayed left, then right, and then stood still after she matched his moves. "I miss knowing who I am and what my place is, but not the lawyering part." He pivoted, took two steps right around her, and was in the air before she could turn.

"Ooooh, very nice." Destiny caught the falling ball and began dribbling around the court, occasionally zigging and zagging around obstacles only she could see. "Like what you're doing?" she said, moving toward the basket.

Earl got between Destiny and the basket, jumped and waved his arms. "It's okay for now. I get a kick out of the kids, and it seems to be leading me into new things."

She was in three-point territory, turned, jumped, and shot. Earl went up and cleanly intercepted the ball, came down, dribbled, took a step, pivoted and went up making the shot. "Where did you pick that up?" Destiny asked, running to get the ball.

"From you, a few minutes ago."

"Oh yeah," she said. "So, where do you think it's leading?"

"Maybe someday I'll actually give you a run for your money," Earl said.

"The job—where is the job at the school leading?" she asked, moving around easily as if she wasn't really playing anymore.

"I don't know, but I feel good about this trip and the PBS special." Earl swooped in and tried to steal the ball. Destiny turned, jumped, and made the three points.

Fist in-the-air she pulled down. "Yes."

Earl shook his head. "Say, will you go to the school and pick up my mail while I'm gone? I leave day after tomorrow."

"Sure."

They hadn't seen the boy approach and only became aware of him when he spoke.

"Hey, Mister, wanna play? Ten dollars if we win."

Earl looked at the tall skinny kid with stick-out ears. "You and who else?"

"My sister," the boy said. "She's pretty good."

Earl laughed. "Sure. Where is she?"

The boy turned and yelled in the direction of a clump of bushes, "Cheryl, come on, they said they'd play."

The two looked as if they might be twins. They were the same size and appeared to be the same age. The girl's interest was clearly in Destiny. "You're pretty good, lady. You ever play for real?"

"A long time ago," Destiny said.

The game was intense. For a short while, Earl and Destiny held their own, but eventually, the kids won.

While Earl paid the boy, Destiny talked with Cheryl. "You're real good. You play on a team?"

The girl nodded.

"Yeah, you're *real* good," Destiny said. "I expect I'll see you again."

Phil Tries a Tofu Burger

Making one of his usual entrances into Mike's Magic Burgers, Phil Reardon bellowed, "Hi ho, Mike. How's it hangin'?"

"Hey, Phil, just the man I wanted to see," Mike said. "I've got a problem. I think you could help me with it."

"Sure, what do you need?"

"A while ago a kid came in and ordered a Tofu Burger. I watched him eat it, and it looked like magic. The kid was a little weird, so I didn't think much about it. But now, other kids are ordering it."

"What's the problem?"

"I need to know why kids order a Tofu Burger," Mike said.

"Are you sure there's no magic?"

"We've been serving it for years, and there was never a hint of magic," Mike said. "A couple of us tried it a few days ago—nothing. But what I see with these kids looks like magic." Mike smiled and shook his head. "The rascals won't tell me about it."

"What do they say?"

"That it's healthy," Mike said.

"Well, that's true."

"And that it tastes good."

"Well, that's nice."

"Really, Phil? Do you believe these kids are coming to Mike's Magic Burgers and eating Tofu Burgers because they're healthy and taste good?"

Phil sniggered. "I guess not. Sure, I'll try one."

Phil made his noisy way across the room. Mike was there with his food as he settled into his seat. "Pay close attention; it may be subtle," Mike said. "And thanks."

Mike watched Phil take a small bite, then a larger one. A broad smile spread across his face. He looked like he was deep in thought, then as if there'd been some revelation. When he'd finished, Mike joined him at his table.

"So?" Mike said.

"It really was good."

"What else?"

"It was like daydreaming. I thought of funny things, like cleaning out my closet, putting up shelves, and I think I have an idea for how to fix a spreadsheet at work—the darn thing's been driving me crazy for days."

Mike looked at his friend. "That sounds too mundane to be magic."

"It may be mundane, but it's also useful. Maybe it helps them study. It sure does taste good. I may have it again myself."

Destiny Coaches

Before he left on his trip, Earl had explained to Destiny where in the school she would find his mail, and that Wednesday would be the best day to pick it up. The first time she went to pick up his mail, she took time to wander the halls of the school. There had been many changes since she'd been a student there. The walls were brighter. The desks were different. But amazingly, it seemed to smell the same.

Walking past the open doors of the gym where she had spent so many hours in her youth, she saw girls playing basketball and stopped to watch. When the woman coaching waved for her to come in, Destiny recognized her as her daughter's friend Darleen Hamilton.

"Ms. Robertson, come in. Come in," Darleen said.

The two sat watching the girls perform their drills. "I never thought I'd be a basketball coach," said the five-foot-four-inch Darleen.

"Are these your regular players?" Destiny asked.

"Some," Darleen said. "In the summer we run practice just for recreation. It keeps the kids busy, out of trouble. Anyone can play. About half these players will make the team."

Destiny watched the girls go through their paces. "You've done a nice job."

"My sport was tennis. I wouldn't mind if you could give me some pointers," Darlene said. Then she stood, blew her whistle, and clapped her hands. "Okay girls, divide into teams."

For the next half hour, Destiny watched the girls play while Darleen instructed. Later, Darleen told them to do a series of stretches and returned to Destiny's side.

"May I?" Destiny said, indicating with her hand that she wanted to go out on the court.

"Sure." Darleen stood up and blew her whistle. The girls turned to face her. "Girls, this is Destiny Robertson. You may have seen her picture in the trophy room. After finishing high school here, she went to Old Dominion. She competed in the International Games—that was before women's basketball was played in the Olympics. Then she played professionally in Europe—because there were no professional women's teams in the United States at that time."

Destiny stepped forward, put her hands in front of her and indicated with a wiggle of her fingers that she wanted the ball. Once she had it, she ran forward, dribbling, and tapped the three largest girls, who followed her to the basket. While the other players moved off the court, Destiny and the three girls formed a circle. She spoke just loudly enough for them to hear.

"It's really tough for tall girls. People are always telling you to watch out for smaller people. We're all big and strong here, so let's show them what we can do when we don't have to watch out for anyone," she said.

At first their moves were awkward, but Destiny was able to give each of them a shot and their success fed on itself. In just a few minutes, they were playing better— more physical, more aggressive. Destiny kept the ball in motion and made sure there were lots of baskets. When they stopped, the others applauded.

Destiny again addressed just the three of them. "That was basketball; remember it. Now, back to the real world. Be careful out there."

"Okay, girls, that's it for today," Darleen yelled, and the girls ran to the locker room. To Destiny she said, "What did you say to them? They looked great!"

A man's voice interrupted. "Ms. Hamilton, your team seems to be coming along nicely. But did I see an unauthorized person on the court?"

"Destiny Robertson, this is Skip Pulchanka, our athletic director," Darleen said, as the tall man approached them.

"Hi, Dee Dee," he said.

"Hi, Skipper," Destiny answered. "You're looking well."

"Thank you, Dee Dee," the man said. "You look well yourself. I'm surprised to see you back in town. How long are you staying?"

"I don't know."

"You never did." Skip's voice had taken on an edge.

"You still got moves, but I can't allow just anyone to work with our students."

He assumed the tall-hands-on-hips stance teachers use to intimidate children. "We have a basketball coach. You see, Dee Dee, while you were off wandering the world, we were in school, learning how to work with children. We are trained, educated, certificated.

"Also, our girls play for recreation. They won't need basketball scholarships to get into college. Their parents expect us to teach them skills appropriate to their status and rank. They don't play the kind of game I know you like."

Destiny knew that all his supposed training had been tender mercies compared to the pressures of being a professional athlete. She could see in the way he stood and hear in his voice that he had matured little over the decades. "Skip, don't you think it's time to let it go?"

For a moment he seemed shocked, as if no one ever spoke back to him. Then his face reddened. His fists clenched, and he took two steps toward her. Destiny maintained her position, stayed calm and relaxed. She was as tall as he, athletic, and unafraid of physical contact. They stood, eye to eye, toe to toe, not moving. His breathing quickened, while Destiny maintained her neutral bearing. Without warning, he turned and stormed out of the gym.

Darleen's eyes were large with fear. "It scared me. You're both so big. It scared me."

"Darleen, this is real old business. It has nothing to do with you," Destiny said. "I'm sorry if I caused you trouble."

Letting go of anger was one of the hardest things Destiny had had to learn as an athlete, but she had learned it well. Even before she'd picked up Earl's mail, the encounter with Skip had been largely forgotten, and she'd moved on to the next part of her day.

On her walk home, she passed the Boys & Girls Club. Cheryl, the girl, who along with her brother had beaten Earl and her a few days earlier, was playing with a group of other girls on the club's outdoor court. Destiny stopped to watch. It was a ragtag looking bunch but with a lot of raw talent and obvious heart.

There had been no one else around when she'd stopped, so she was surprised to hear a man's voice close behind her say, "They've got spunk."

Turning, she saw a dark, stocky, mustached man, substantially shorter than her. "Who are they?" Destiny asked.

"Homeschoolers and troublemakers, mostly." He gave Destiny a quick once-over. "You play?"

"Used to," she said.

"College?"

Destiny nodded. "Old Dominion."

The man put out his hand. "Tony Martino. I've been working with the girls."

"Destiny Robertson."

His face lit with recognition. "You played…"

"A long time ago," Destiny said.

"In Europe too."

Destiny nodded.

"Do you have time?" he asked, extending his arm toward the gate. "Come in. It would mean a lot to the girls."

"Actually, I played Cheryl about a week ago. She's good," Destiny said.

"She and her brother take some money off you?"

"Yup."

"They'll do that. They're both good."

Destiny allowed him to lead her onto the court, where he introduced her. The girls listened attentively to what she said and then asked her to show them things. Just like that, she was coaching.

"Ladies! We've got to stop now," Tony said, an hour later.

"Aw, just a little bit longer," several girls moaned.

"Your moms are lined up in front, getting impatient. Thank Ms. Robertson for her help."

"Thank you, Ms. Robertson," they chorused. "Will you come again?" a couple asked.

Destiny looked at Tony.

"I'll try to talk her into it. Now, you ladies get going, or your mothers are going to be mad." Turning to Destiny, he said, "I could use the help."

"I have no teaching credentials," Destiny said.

"That's not an issue. You're good with the kids. You know the game. Oh, and I'm not going to pay you. See you Friday?"

"Sure," she said.

Daphne's Decorating Decision

Saturday evening, a disheveled Daphne Miller walked into Mike's Magic Burgers. She wore faded, paint-splattered jeans, a sweatshirt, and tennis shoes with holes at the toes. She smelled of paint and sweat.

"Wow," Mike said. "You're always so put together when you come in for lunch. I'd have guessed you didn't own a sweatshirt."

"I bought a house, and the inside has to be painted before I move in. No big deal, right? Well, do you know what painters cost? Having started it myself, I can see why they charge so much! I'm beat. I could use some love from the universe. Can I have a Special Burger?"

Mike looked sheepish. "Oh, no! I'm out of sauce. It's one of the herbs—no one has any. I'm sorry."

"Darn. I looked forward to it all day!"

"Let's see, what would be a good substitute?" Mike said. "Do you know how you're going to decorate?"

Daphne shook her head. "I'm having trouble making up my mind."

"Okay, a Decision Burger, on the house—to celebrate your new house." Mike gave her one of his smiles. "You know the drill. Have a seat, and it'll be ready in a flash,"

She had just gotten comfortable in her usual booth, when Mike arrived with her meal. "Enjoy."

She lifted the burger in both hands, closed her eyes, and took a bite. When she opened them, she was in the hall of what appeared to be a government building—certainly not a place where a trendy decorator would have a studio. A woman with pursed lips and two pair of glasses hanging around her neck sat behind a green metal desk, looking at her.

"May I help you?" she asked.

"I'm here to make some decorating decisions," Daphne said.

The woman turned her head, revealing a tight bun low on her head. Raising her left arm, she pointed down the hall. "Room D."

"Thank you," Daphne said. Turning, she rolled her eyes and wondered what sort of decorator would be in a building like this, with a receptionist like that, at such an ugly old desk. Entering the room, she hoped to see a skinny, otherworldly sort of person with outrageous hair and big jewelry—or maybe some body piercings. She was disappointed to find a rumpled, loose-skinned, older man sitting behind a distressed metal desk, (very like the one in the hall) filing his nails. Adding to her dismay were the career-counseling books on the shelves and certificates on the wall.

"I came for help making a decorating decision," Daphne said.

The man looked up. "Oh, come in. Sit down. Decorating, you said?" He went to each of the bookcases and touched a corner. The regular-size books changed to large picture books with titles featuring various decorating styles, and decorating magazines collected in holders. Swatches of fabric and carpet samples appeared hanging from sturdy hooks along the walls. He went to the diplomas and turned them over so decorating credentials were visible. As he walked around, pictures of extravagantly decorated rooms and rolls of blue-prints appeared.

Settling into his chair, he made a sweeping motion with his arm, and the wall behind him transformed into a window, overlooking a golf course. "There, now we can begin."

"I just bought a house," Daphne said. "I'm having trouble deciding what style I want to decorate."

"What do you like?" the man asked.

"Southwestern. But my sister thinks it's awful, and the New York magazines say it's passé."

"Who will live in the house?" the man asked.

"Me."

"Who will pay for the house?"

"Me."

"What do you like?" the man asked.

"Southwestern…"

The man raised his hand to stop her. "Visit your sister at her house. And next time a New York magazine wants to do a story about you, meet the interviewer at a restaurant—which is always a good idea since they're likely to criticize just about anything. Any other questions?"

"Should I use a decorator or do it myself?" Daphne said.

"Have you ever decorated before?" the man asked.

"No."

"Do you have any special artistic knack?"

"I'm not bad. But, well, no."

"Is it important how it looks?"

"Uh, that's why I'm taking time to think about it."

"Use a decorator," the man said.

"What about the money? How do you know I can afford a decorator?"

"Doesn't matter," the man said. "Since you said it was important how it looked, I figured that if you made a mistake, you'd correct it. People who are decorating for the first time almost always make at least one mistake. So a decorator could save you money, since it is more likely to be done right in the first place."

"Thanks," Daphne said without enthusiasm.

"My pleasure," the man said. Then he opened the desk drawer, took out his nail file, and returned to his manicure.

Daphne closed her eyes on the decorator's studio and opened them back in the restaurant. Mike sat across from her.

"Any good?" Mike asked.

"I'm not sure," Daphne said.

Mike looked disappointed. "Didn't it help?"

"It actually was good advice. But it was just common sense."

"Yeah." Mike nodded. "A lot of magic is."

Kids...

On her way in to coach, Destiny dropped the envelope containing Earl's accumulated correspondence in the mailbox in front of the Boys & Girls Club. Included was a letter from Laura Witherspoon. She thought that would likely be important to him.

Destiny paid no particular attention to the mothers who attended the girls' basketball practice on her first official day of coaching.

When the girls finished playing, Tony Martino pulled Destiny aside. "I didn't mention it before because I thought it would make you nervous. But your presence raised concerns among some of the girls' mothers." He nodded toward the bleachers. "They want to talk to you."

The leader of the group stepped forward. "Miss Robertson, you seem to be a fine coach."

"Thank you," Destiny said.

Tony stood slightly behind Destiny and spoke softly. "Ms. Robertson, Mrs. Samuels is Cheryl's mother. She wanted to meet you."

"Mrs. Samuels, it's a pleasure to meet you. Your daughter is a very talented athlete, and so is your son—I met them at the park."

"Miss Robertson, I won't mince words," Mrs. Samuels said. "All of us are concerned about our children. A bunch of us homeschool because we have ideas outside the mainstream, which we do not want challenged. Some of the girls have had unpleasant experiences in the public education system. We are careful who we allow into their lives."

Destiny smiled. "I understand your concern. I have a daughter myself. I wanted her to be an artist or a performer. I exposed her to the freest thinkers, the finest minds in Europe and the United States. She went to the most progressive schools on both continents. I wanted her to be aware of all the options in the world so she could choose the most interesting life possible.

"You can imagine my surprise when she chose to pursue a graduate degree in business administration. Today she is a CPA in a town twenty miles from here. Her husband is a plumbing contractor, and they hope to have a large family. I love her dearly, but I am more than a little surprised by her life choices."

"A CPA is an accountant, right?" Mrs. Samuels said.

Destiny nodded.

Mrs. Samuels smiled broadly. "An accountant? All that other stuff, and she decides to be an accountant. You're okay with that?"

"She's my daughter. I'm okay with whatever she decides as long as it's legal and won't hurt her."

Mrs. Samuels turned to Tony Martino, whose face was red from holding his breath. "She'll be fine."

To Destiny, she said, "The girls sure like you."

Mrs. Samuels began to take her leave, but then stopped and turned. "It's a small town, Ms. Robertson. I know about you and Skip Pulchanka. You don't have to worry about that."

Mrs. Samuels chuckled as she and the other women left. "An accountant. Isn't that just the way? She takes the kid all over the world, and she ends up an accountant in a small town," she said.

Tony looked at Destiny, "Is that story about your daughter true?"

"Yes," Destiny said.

"What's the Pulchanka stuff?"

"Until a couple of days ago, I thought it was ancient history, never to be retold. But now it seems like something you may want to know." Destiny sighed. "Skip and I were in high school together—both of us won basketball scholarships to attend college—different schools. In our sophomore year, we were home visiting for Christmas. The principal of the high school invited the two of us to speak at an assembly—to tell the students about our experiences.

"The coach picked each of us up at our homes. On the way to the school, there was an accident. Skip was badly hurt. His injuries meant he could never go pro. I didn't have a scratch on me. There was a feeling, rather openly expressed, that if one of the kids had to be hurt, it was too bad it was him. After all, what was a girl athlete going to do anyway?"

"I'm sorry," Tony said, his expression pained. "That's awful. Hearing that must have hurt you terribly. But that was a long time ago. Things have changed a lot since then."

"Not for Skip."

John Tries a Tofu Burger

Mike was cleaning the sinks when he heard someone walk into the restaurant. From where he stood, he could only see the chest of the man who entered, but the blue coverall with *Chuck* embroidered over the pocket was enough for him to know who it was. "John, I'll be there in a second," he yelled. The boy stood at the order counter when he walked out of the kitchen a few minutes later. "Sorry to keep you waiting. How's it going?" he said.

"Good," John said, smiling. "I'm working on something really tricky. It's my favorite thing."

Mike liked the boy. "Would you try a Tofu Burger for me and tell me what it's like?"

"Sure," the boy said. "I thought there wasn't any magic in a Tofu Burger."

"I thought that too," Mike said. "But lately, college students are coming in and ordering it."

"Have you asked them?"

"Sure," Mike said. "They tell me it's healthy and tastes good. But, well, you know how the magic gives people that sort of dreamy look? The kids have that."

John nodded. "Sure, I'll try it. Why not?"

Mike brought the burger to John's table. "Pay extra attention so you can tell me about it."

Mike stood behind the counter watching John eat. He thought the young man looked unusually content. Satisfied. It looked sort of like magic—but different too. It looked like he was thinking about things—like when a dog twitches in his sleep. He figured John could give him the straight story.

When the boy opened, his eyes Mike sat across from him. "What happened?" Mike asked.

"There's no magic; it's a Tofu Burger," he said, and then laughed grinning mischievously.

This sort of silliness was uncharacteristic for John.

"Tell me what happened," Mike said. "I need to know. I'm responsible."

John laughed again. "Okay. But really, there's not much to tell. It's not like the other burgers. I feel rested—almost as if I've had a nap. I figured out how to fix that tricky problem I told you about, and now I wanna get back to the shop while it's still fresh. Oh, and I feel, happy—very, very happy." The boy stood to leave. "Mike, it really does taste good."

Mike knew that at the very least, he'd have to change the description on the menu. But what was he going to say? It sounded too mundane to be magic.

Dinner with Destiny's Daughter

Destiny was preparing dinner in her daughter, Coleen's, tiny kitchen. She liked cooking. It soothed her. Her hands and the air smelled of garlic. While she worked, she half listened to Coleen explaining a new bookkeeping program to Dee in the next room.

"I may be too old to learn computer accounting stuff," Dee said. "How do you close the period? How do I get reports?"

"Gram, you're doing fine. It just seems confusing because it's new. In this program you only close at year end, but you can print out quarterly reports. Imagine all the numbers are just sitting there, waiting for you to ask for them in any format you want. The rules are still the same: assets minus liabilities still equals net worth, and net worth still equals opening equity plus profits minus owner's draw. So owner's draw can be a separate equity account that directly offsets the others. See?"

"You're skipping a step," Dee said.

"Yeah." The young woman nodded, smiling. "You got it."

"What about year end?"

"Close the draw account into the opening equity," Coleen said.

"What about profits?"

"Automatic."

"Really? That's cool," Dee said. "Are you sure?"

"Yup, Grandma. I'm sure."

Destiny yelled, "Dinner's almost ready. Are we going to wait for Scott?" and the back door opened.

"I'm here!" Coleen's husband stood outside on the step. His overalls were splattered with muck, and an unpleasant odor came into the room through the open door. "A major sewer line broke," he said. "The city called a few of us contractors in to help."

"Oh, Scott, you smell terrible," Coleen said. "Get out of those clothes. Shower in the backyard, and leave your stuff outside."

"Thanks, sweetie." He leaned forward, puckered his lips, and made a loud smacking noise in the air.

Coleen smiled. "Okay, you romantic devil, hurry, dinner's ready. Mom cooked, so it will be an unusual treat for you."

Dee and Destiny watched Scott go to the backyard shower enclosure while Coleen made a quick trip through the house, getting him clean sweats and a towel. Coleen knew just where to put his dry things, and Scott appeared to have a system for rinsing his gear then throwing it, so it landed on the lawn just right. It appeared this was a well-practiced maneuver.

"I'm hurrying," he yelled.

Coleen was laughing when she came back into the kitchen.

"He's a real cutie," Destiny said.

Coleen nodded. "Fun too."

Scott came in smelling of strong soap, his wet hair combed straight back. "Okay, the man's here, the meal can be served," he said, standing tall with his chest thrust out, as if making a proclamation.

Coleen wrinkled her face. "Are you sure you can eat after that stink?"

"No man would let a little thing like a few hundred gallons of raw sewage stop him from enjoying one of your mother's meals."

Destiny shook her head. She freely admitted that her daughter had found a wonderful husband. "Okay, Mr. Charm, I suppose that means you want the rarest meat, of which there is less than usual, because of the delay."

"Destiny, you know how to treat a man. If I weren't married to your daughter..."

"And you were twenty years older," Destiny said.

"That wouldn't matter to me," Scott said. "Say it wouldn't matter to you, either."

Destiny shook her head. "Okay, Okay, you've got the rare part."

Scott put his fist in the air and pulled down. "Yes."

As they started to eat, Coleen turned to Destiny. "Mom, are you starting a cooking class?"

"Yeah. Did you see the catalog?" Destiny asked.

"Did the blurb look okay? I haven't seen it."

"It looked fine, Mom," Coleen said. "I hear you're also coaching the girls' basketball team at the Boys & Girls Club."

"Yeah. There's some real talent there," Destiny said. "There's this one girl, Cheryl—she could be real good. Real good. Yesterday…"

Dee's chuckle cut Destiny short. "Dee Dee, I think Coleen wants to know if you intend to stay around for a while."

Destiny looked surprised. "Oh." She turned to Coleen. "Is that what you're asking?"

Coleen nodded.

"I thought it was obvious," Destiny said.

"Is that a yes?" Coleen asked.

"Will you continue to stay with me?" Dee asked.

"Yes," Destiny said. Feeling self-consciousness, she added. "If it's okay. I know you're used to being on your own."

"It's more than okay, Dee Dee. I love having you here," Dee said. "But some of us verbalize our plans to people they might affect."

Destiny felt her cheek twitch. "Maybe I've been alone a little too long."

Dee leaned over to the chair next to hers and hugged her daughter. "Maybe you have."

Scott seized the floor. "Well, now that we've settled that, I've got to tell you about that sewer line. You think I was a mess—that was nothing. I wasn't even soaked through. Bruce had a tiny hole in his suit. Yuck, was he a mess. Then there was this house, they'd just finished a big remodel—it's ruined—what a waste. We saved a dog—that was a close one. Poor little thing. It's going to take some scrubbing to get that smell off him. And there was this one guy who wouldn't leave his house without his TV. Can you imagine risking your health for a TV?"

Listening to her son-in-law, Destiny knew that tomorrow the sewer line break would be a front-page story, full of angst, tragedy, property damage, and health risks. There would be pictures of local residents wailing their dismay and terror to anyone who would listen—and to the world at large, if there was no one to listen. A counseling site might be set up for those who experienced the trauma of the broken sewer line.

But at her daughter's house, one of the main workers on the scene laughed with his family about the terrible mess and how bad it smelled, while he enjoyed a meal cooked by his mother-in-law.

After having ice cream for dessert, they played Scrabble.

Going National

Seeing Hinckley walk into the restaurant, Maria marked her place and closed the book she was reading.

"Sorry to be late. I had trouble getting away," Hinckley said, sliding into the other side of the booth. "The message I got didn't make any sense. It said you were reopening Chicken Shit and wanted an operating line."

"That was the message." Maria nodded. "I guessed it might be confusing." She smiled.

"You're CEO of Animal World. What's going on?"

"I didn't intend to be coy, though I guess it must seem so." Maria smiled. "As you know, Animal World is on the brink of a public offering that will allow it to expand into a national chain. I am helping with public relations, but it has been made clear to the financial world that professional management has taken over everyday operations. I will be kept on as a consultant, receive a generous retainer, and should anyone ever call me, a huge fee."

"They're pushing you out?" Hinckley took Maria's hands in his. "This is terrible. I'm so sorry this is happening to you."

She shook her head. "No, Hinckley, this is great! A big chunk of my stock will be sold in the public offering. I have what I wanted. You know, I loved my little store. What got to me was never having enough money. I couldn't afford health insurance or car repairs. Every expense was an opera. I had to do something. After this stock sale, I will be rich enough to be able to enjoy the wonderful life I used to have."

"Doesn't it hurt to be thrown out of your own company?"

Maria shrugged. "It isn't my company anymore. The minute I brought in the business types, they started taking credit for everything. They acted like the whole idea—the store, the departments, the going public—all of it, was their plan. It was my plan. I still have one of the original binders. But they claim all the credit. They talk to me as if I'm a child. I'll be happy if I never have to talk to any of them ever again."

"Maria, this may not be the right time for this," Hinckley said. "But I've always found you attractive and interesting and wanted to ask you out."

Maria smiled. "But you couldn't because I was a customer of the bank."

Hinckley shook his head. "Oh, bankers don't have rules like that. No, it just wasn't a good time for me. I'm ready now. Would you…?"

Mike walked by their table. "You two eating today?"

Maria smiled at Hinckley. "Want to take a walk on the beach?"

He nodded eagerly.

"We'll have Tropical Burgers."

The Big Game

Every year at the beginning of the season, the high school girls' basketball team played a game against the Boys & Girls Club team for practice. Most years the high school team won. But under Destiny Robertson's leadership, the Boys & Girls Club team was ahead. Like most coaches, Destiny was happy to be able to give the second-string players court time in a real game, and hers were doing a good job maintaining the fifteen-point lead.

Late in the second half, Mrs. Samuels approached her. "There's a recruiter here."

"How do you know?" Destiny asked.

"I was sitting behind Mr. Pulchanka—from the high school. I heard him talking. The recruiter just got here. Miss Robertson, my Cheryl needs a scholarship, and the only one she'll ever get is basketball."

"I understand."

Destiny returned her starters to the floor. Within minutes, Cheryl had made a basket and drawn the foul. As the Boys & Girls Club team scored again and again, the excitement grew. By the end of the game, the crowd was on their feet watching the homeschoolers and troublemakers, in their not-quite-matching uniforms, win by forty-five points.

Skip Pulchanka looked fierce when he approached Destiny after the game. "That was uncalled for," he said. "How did you know he was here?"

"Who?"

"You know who—the recruiter."

"There was a recruiter here? Really? That can't be so—you'd have told me," Destiny said. "After all, your girls don't need basketball scholarships. That's what you said, isn't it? You know mine do—you'd have told me if there was a recruiter here. No, it must be that tonight I just wanted my girls see what it feels like to trounce another team."

Too keyed up to go home after the game, Destiny stopped at Mike's. She was surprised and happy to see Earl there and slid into the booth across from him. "When did you get back?"

"A little while ago," Earl said. "How'd your game go?"

Destiny smiled. "We won—by forty-five points. I know it's bad form, but there was a recruiter there. Skip Pulchanka didn't tell me. My girls need scholarships.

When I found out about the recruiter, I just turned 'em loose and let 'em wail. We whooped 'em! It was great."

Remembering her manners, she asked, "How was your trip?"

Earl's thoughtfulness was in stark contrast to Destiny's excitement. "Interesting," he said. "I never realized how idealistic people are; most genuinely want to do a job that is meaningful. Person after person told us they wanted to help the needy, heal the sick, fix the broken, defend the innocent, do something to make the world a better place. They told us stories about people who epitomize their ideal. To bankers, especially on the West Coast, A. P. Giannini was a favorite. Attorneys mentioned Abraham Lincoln and William Kunstler. Mechanics mentioned a relative or friend who could fix things or this guy, Tesla, who I'd never heard of."

"Before, did you think you were the only one?" Destiny asked.

Earl nodded. "Not the only one, but different, yeah. But that's all wrong. Other people we talked to started out just like me with the genuine belief they would be able to change the world, at least a little. When they realized the constraints of the job wouldn't allow that, they stayed in order to make money. Most thought they'd be able to change back to something with meaning later, after the baby started school, and the car or house were paid off. Every time they thought about making a change, there was a new financial crisis to stop them. Little by little, they gave up the ideal and decided they just needed to keep slogging along, doing a job that never would become the work they hoped to accomplish.

They needed the money. It was the same story over and over.

"The kids I traveled with heard it. One of them asked me if anyone ended up with the life they planned."

"What did you say?"

"I said that I was wondering the same thing myself."

"There must have been people who just wanted money," Destiny said.

"Oh sure," Earl said. "We found clusters of them in the big companies. They didn't talk about what they could do for the world. They talked about their willingness to do what had to be done. The way they talked, it sounded as if flattery was their most useful talent, and networking was their major skill—not special insights or talent, not special anything, just a willingness to do passable work and talk to people about it."

"Will this insight change your videos?" Destiny asked.

"Maybe. I have to think about how to use it," Earl said. "Now the videos are just information—they address the nuts and bolts of the job. They are for youngsters making their initial career choice. I think we could add depth and address the reasons, other than money, why people work. We could present to older people, like me, looking at a second or third career. We've got skills and savings. This is a chance to remember our dreams and pursue them."

"Did you meet any people who'd done that?" Destiny asked.

"Yeah," Earl said. "They were interesting. They talked less than the others, but they had a way about them.

They were calm, sure, and comfortable with themselves."

The combination of her excitement over winning the game and an earnest conversation with a decent-looking guy, made Destiny feel like a young girl. She realized she was…horny.

While Earl talked, he had been looking down at his hands and the table in front of him. Now he looked at Destiny and he became awkward. She could tell from his reaction that her inclination must be obvious.

"Want a burger?" she asked.

Earl looked uncomfortable. "Oooookay. Sure. A burger."

Destiny caught Mike's eye. "Bring us a couple Special Burgers."

Mike smiled and said, "Sorry, no Special Burgers on the first date."

Destiny was incredulous. "Mike, we're not kids. This is ridiculous. I made the first Special Sauce."

"Yes, and you also helped make the rules," Mike said. "One of the rules is, 'No Special Burgers on a first date.'"

"Mike!"

He put his hands on his hips, his eyebrows arched. "Another is 'Rules are rules.' Sorry, Destiny."

"Okay, we'll have Tropical Burgers. But we don't need suits."

"Not my call, Destiny. You know the magic decides."

Fishy Burger Deluxe

Daphne had loved the Fishy Burger and intended, from the minute she finished it, to try the Fishy Burger Deluxe, but she'd gotten distracted by work things and then buying the house and making decorating decisions. Looking up at the menu at Mike's Magic Burgers she remembered her intention; and that's what she ordered.

She went to her usual booth. Shortly, Mike slid the plate in front of her. "Enjoy."

"I will," she thought, lifting the sandwich, closing her eyes, and taking a bite. Opening her eyes she found herself beside the rusting glacier-blue, '55 Chevy, parked in the seaweed forest, same as before. Looking around, it seemed the fish were the same too.

A largish fish stopped in front of her, and stared at her with his fish eyes. She recognized him as one who had helped her the last time and performed a few maneuvers, to show him (and herself) that she didn't need help. She told him she remembered what he'd shown her. But his face remained expressionless, and she could only hope he understood how much she appreciated his previous help. Then he winked and swam off, leaving her smiling and waving at his tail.

Swimming into the car, she saw the yellow striped fish and joined them in swimming back and forth. They were friendly and gave her a place in their formation. As nice and inviting as they were, she tired of the repetitiveness of their back-and-forth swimming. Shortly, she bid them ado.

The orange fish approached and stopped suddenly by her side. She stayed perfectly still, which she knew was their way, and then started up suddenly to swim madly for a short distance, only to stop suddenly again. This required both skill and a sort of intuition, but ultimately it too failed to hold her attention.

Seeing the blue-and-green fish in the distance, she excused herself and joined them. They played tag, follow the leader, kick the algae, tease the anemone, and terrorize the black striped fish. It was all great fun.

She closed her eyes to laugh about the adventure, and found herself back at Mike's.

"Like it?" he asked.

She giggled. "I get it—with the Deluxe Burger, you get to kiss them back."

The Morning After

Dee stood in her kitchen waiting for the last of the coffee to drip into the pot. A bag from the local bakery sat on the counter. When Destiny walked in, she spoke sharply to her. "Dee Dee, I appreciate that you were probably trying to be discreet by not spending the night with Earl, but you woke me when you came in."

"Sorry, Mom," Destiny said, sheepishly.

Dee's face and voice softened. "I wouldn't have guessed Earl could put such a big grin on anyone's face."

"It's been a while." Destiny blushed. "To be honest, I wasn't trying to be discreet. I couldn't sleep with him. I'm not used to sharing a bed, and I'm too old to miss a night's sleep."

"I can't imagine Earl getting up the gumption to ask you," Dee said.

"We were in Mike's," Destiny said. "I'd won the game—by a lot—there seemed to be quite a bit of random magic in the air. Oh, heck, *he* didn't get up the gumption; it was me. I'm not even sure he wanted to."

Dee nodded. "I'd guess by the look on your face, he got into the spirit."

"Yes, he did."

"I see what you like in him—he has potential," Dee said. "But remember all those possibilities are wrapped in the body and mind of Earl Witherspoon, a man who, by my reckoning, still has several major decisions to make, including what he's going to do about his marriage."

Destiny groaned. "I thought that was done. I thought they were separated."

"Living apart is a better description," Dee said.

Destiny groaned again. "I didn't realize. They've been apart so long. I assumed…"

Dee shook her head. "They still have unfinished business."

"I thought they were further along. He didn't say anything."

Dee looked sympathetic.

"He seemed ready," Destiny said.

"To know Destiny?" Dee said. "Few men are ever ready for that."

"Darn. It was nice to be with someone."

"I know you get lonely," Dee said. "But I think you'll have to throw this one back."

"Mom…"

Dee interrupted. "I don't like to meddle, but…"

"Of course you do; that's why you read palms."

"Don't interrupt while I'm meddling," Dee said, and

the two women laughed.

"Earl is not ready for you, Dee Dee. I'm afraid you'll get hurt. He's probably watching us right now from his window, too scared to come over and have coffee. Men are never at their best when they're scared. You don't know what he might say or do."

"Mom, you never thought any man was good enough for me."

"That's my job; now let me finish. Take care of yourself, because he's going to take care of himself. To him, you are an experienced woman. He won't think twice about your feelings. He'll worry about himself—and if the issue arises—his wife."

"So you think it was a mistake?" Destiny said.

"Only you can answer that. Have a sticky roll and pass me one."

The women went on to discuss their plans for the day. After Dee left the house, Earl came into the kitchen. "Does she know?"

"Yeah," Destiny said.

"What did she say?"

"That I should be more quiet when I come in." Destiny looked at the anxious Earl. "Have you been sitting and watching us, waiting for Mom to leave so you could come over?"

"Of course I waited for her to leave," Earl said. "Is she angry at me?"

"For what?"

Earl could barely form words. "Yyyyyou knooow."

Destiny saw that her mother had been right in her evaluation of Earl. "You mean like, 'You spoiled my daughter'?"

Earl threw his hands up in the air. "I knew she was mad. She's been a wonderful friend. She let me live in her home, and this is what I do."

"Earl, she is not angry with you," Destiny said.

Earl whined. "I've betrayed her. She helped me, opened her home to me, and I seduced her daughter."

Destiny realized how completely she'd misjudged him. "She's not angry with you. She is concerned that I might get hurt, but she is not angry."

"You, get hurt?" Earl said. "If anyone is likely to get hurt, it's me. You're single. You've done this before. I've been married most of my adult life. What do I know about this?"

Destiny looked at Earl's guileless face and felt her stomach sink. After he left, she finished the coffee and ate the last sticky roll.

Long Hot Walk

As usual, Phil Reardon cheerfully greeted everyone he saw as he walked into Mike's Magic Burgers. Approaching the counter, he bellowed, "Hey, Mike, how's tricks?" A thin, pale man, who was a head shorter and seventy-five pounds lighter than him, stood at his side. "This is my friend Alan. We work together. I've been trying to get him here for months. We'll have Oasis Burgers."

Mike smiled. "Phil, not everyone appreciates the Oasis Burger like you do. But just about everyone likes the Tropical Burger. Maybe that would be a better choice for his first time."

Phil waved aside Mike's concern, "I've thoroughly briefed him; he's up for it." Phil put his arm around his friend's shoulder. "Isn't that right, buddy? You're up for this, right?"

"Really?" Alan said. "It's pretty hard to believe the

magic stuff. I mean if it's true I'll be astonished. To be honest I'm just hoping for a decent burger."

Mike gave Phil a questioning look.

"It'll be okay," Phil said. "He knows what to expect. I'll be with him."

Mike shrugged. "Okay. Two Oasis Burgers, coming up."

Phil led the way across the restaurant, introducing Alan to a half dozen people along the way. Once they were seated, Mike slid the burgers in front of them. "Enjoy."

"Now remember what I told you," Phil said to Alan. "Close your eyes and take a big bite. Ready?"

Alan, his lip curled in a smirk, nodded. Each man closed his eyes and took a bite of his burger. Opening his eyes on the other side, Phil could see the shock on his friend's face. "Hey, buddy, isn't it great?"

Alan looked around and then at Phil. "We're in a desert!"

"Yeah, beautiful, isn't it? See the view?"

"Where's the oasis?"

"Up there." Phil pointed up the canyon. "You can just see the palm trees up the hill."

"How do we get there?" Alan said, with panic in his voice.

"Walk. You'll love it. The plants are great." Phil began the uphill trek. "But don't touch any of them. Some have thorns, and others have little sticky things that will get into your skin and make it itch. Come on, this way."

Alan was sweating before they even got to the place where the trail started to climb up the hill, and winded by the time Phil stooped to sing to a small barrel cactus. His discordant voice echoed through the canyon. "You are fine and noble and a delight to my eyes. Your growth gives strength to my soul. Praise be to God."

Phil continued walking up the hill, singing to the plants, as he liked to do. "Oh, century plant; oh, century plant, what a heroic plant you are."

Phil stopped, giving his sweat-soaked and panting coworker the opportunity to catch up. "Look over there. That's where the coyotes live."

It was a short stop. Phil marched on, continuing to share his knowledge without looking to see if Alan was interested or even near enough to hear him—oblivious to his friend's discomfort. "See this plant? There's another over there. See? About twelve feet away. They're most likely connected through their roots. One is the offspring of the other. And that one over there? Next month it will have tiny red flowers on it. We'll have to come back so you can see it."

Reaching the oasis, Phil stripped down, walked into the small pond, went down on his knees, then belly flopped into the shallow water.

Alan arrived several minutes later and, surveying the scene, looked incredulous. "This is it? We walked all that way for this?"

"Isn't it great? Come on in." Phil was confused by the look on his friend's face. "It's great. Isn't it?"

Returning to Mike's, Phil heard Alan's angry words, "I can't believe anyone would deliberately walk miles, uphill, in the desert, to splash around in a mud puddle. It was awful!" Alan got up from the table and left the restaurant.

Phil looked at Mike and was, for a rare moment, speechless.

Mike put his hand on Phil's. "Some people enjoy the walk, and others don't."

"Maybe," Phil said. "But the magic—how could he not be amazed by the magic?"

"That's something I ask all the time."

Destiny's in Iowa

A doleful Earl faced Mike across the order counter of Mike's Magic Burgers. "I don't know what to do," he whined.

"What happened?" Mike said.

"Beth called last night." Earl said. "The conversation started nice. She told me how sweet it was for me to try to get closer to Laura, my older daughter. But then one thing led to another, and she told me she was going out for pizza with some professor."

When Mike didn't comment, Earl repeated himself. "Beth—my wife—is having pizza with another man."

Mike shrugged. "You've been living apart for quite a while. And aren't you seeing Destiny?"

"That's different," Earl said. "Anyway, she's in Iowa at a women's basketball thing."

"But that's only for a week."

"She's going to stop on the way back to sell books,"

Earl said.

Mike nodded. "Yes, but then she comes home. Then you see her."

"But she's not here now," Earl said. "My wife is having pizza with another man, and I'm all alone."

"Have you talked to Destiny?"

Earl raised his voice. "You don't know what this is like. The mother of my children is seeing another man, and I'm all alone. Destiny isn't here. I'm all alone."

Mike inhaled loudly. "Earl, I'm not the right one to talk to about this. You should talk to Dee."

"Are you kidding?" Earl said. "I seduced her daughter. She invited me into her house, and I seduced her daughter."

"Maybe you should call Destiny," Mike said. "Or why don't you fly to Iowa?"

"I can't just leave. I have things to do," Earl said.

"Or maybe talk to Harvey," Mike said.

"But…" Earl stopped, when Coleen came into the restaurant carrying a cloth bag with fresh herbs sticking out the top. She walked around the counter, and kissed Mike on the cheek. "Hi Dad. Gram asked me to drop this off."

"Coleen," Mike said. "Have you met Earl? Earl," he said. "This is Coleen. Destiny's and my daughter."

Earl's body twitched. Then he mumbled something unintelligible and left.

"What was that?" Coleen asked.

"A man in overload," Mike answered.

"Is he the guy from Grandma's guesthouse?"

Mike nodded.

"Mom spend time with him?"

Mike nodded again.

"Mom has that effect on some people," Coleen said.

"Yes, she does. But I think Earl goes into overload all on his own over pretty much everything." He felt one of the leaves sticking out of the bag, broke it off its stem, and then tasted it. "The basil is perfect."

Catherine Tells

Saturday night, Mike stood behind the order counter to watch Catherine and John finish their Tofu Burgers. When it was clear they were done, he approached their table. They opened their eyes and smiled at each other. John raised Catherine's hand to his lips. Mike's voice startled them.

"You've got to tell me what it's like," he said.

"Mike, I already told you," John said.

"Try to see this from my perspective. I run a restaurant that sells magic burgers. Suddenly I've got a burger that is not supposed to be magic become very popular with young people—couples. I feel responsible."

John glared at him. "It's just nice, and it's healthy and it tastes good."

"Please. I need to know," Mike pleaded.

Catherine squeezed John's hand. "I understand. The police already watch him because of the Special Burger."

"They do?" John said.

"Yeah, my dad comes in here regularly and gives him a hard time," Catherine said.

"He does?" John said.

Mike's eyes opened wide. "You're Chet's daughter?"

Catherine turned to Mike. "Don't worry. My great-grandmother told me my dad just has a bug about my great-grandfather dying and all—but that it wasn't your fault."

John looked at Catherine. "Your great-grandfather? What is this about?"

"I'll explain it later. Right now I think we should tell Mike what happens. He needs to know."

When John didn't say anything, she started talking. "It's different every time, but it's always nice—personal. This time it was as if we were married. We have a house in the burbs—it's little but brand new—and we have one child, and I'm pregnant with a second. I don't work, so I have time to plant a garden and sew and stuff like that. We're not rich, but we don't have to worry. This time John came home with a brand-new car, and we went for a ride."

It took Mike a while to realize she'd finished. "It's like that every time? Sort of a light daydream?"

Catherine nodded. "Yeah, more or less. Once I was in a training program put on by my employer. The HR woman told me the company believed I was valuable and wanted me to be loyal. I was well paid, and I had health insurance and a retirement plan. Once I even got a promotion."

Mike looked at John. "So you told me the truth.

There is no magic. What's the attraction?"

"A new house. A new car. On-the-job-training," John said.

"But that's not magic," Mike said.

"Maybe not for you," John said.

Mike looked at the two young faces and felt humble. He'd forgotten that magic, like beauty, is in the eye of the beholder.

Video Kings

Midweek, midafternoon, Earl and Dee were the only people in Mike's Magic Burgers. Earl's concern that Dee might be angry with him had been outweighed by his need to tell someone about what was happening. As usual, Dee listened while Earl talked.

"Dee, things are moving so fast. It's happening—the videos are going to be on PBS. Pete and Les want to go into business making and selling these things. Doug, an old friend of mine, is perfect to help with the business and legal end. They want me to organize and do the interviews. They're meeting me here."

"I hear you're moving back into your house?" Dee asked.

"It's incredible," Earl said. "The day we started talking about the business and where we'd put it, my tenant called, saying he'd been transferred and asking if he could end the lease early. The timing is perfect for me.

We can work there and not need to rent a place until we get rolling. The painters are at the house now. The furniture will come out of storage at the end of the week."

"How do you feel about all this?" Dee said.

"It'll be great to have a real business again," Earl said.

"Like your law practice," Dee said.

"This is different—creative. I have some ideas about the videos. I want to add depth to all of them and then edit them and have a separate version aimed at older people. I'm not sure if you realize that most people don't want to just work for money. They want to do something to help people. This can be my second chance to do something important."

"Earl, this is like your law practice. You and three other guys in business. You thought you'd be providing a valuable service, but then something changed. Have you figured out what went wrong in your law practice?

"Bill retired."

"You were unhappy before that."

"Just because it's me and three other guys doesn't mean it's like my law practice. And anyway, that was pretty good. I may have been a little restless—but it was all right until Bill retired. That was what changed. I've taken time to think about this. I really know what I want."

"You and these three guys are going to have a regular business that is completely different from the law practice you used to have with three other guys."

"Dee..." Seeing the three men walk in, Earl left his sentence unfinished.

While the men made their way across the room, Dee wrote something on a piece of paper, handed it to Earl, and said, "We'll talk later." Earl nodded and put the paper in his pocket, watching her walk away.

The three men joined Earl at his table. Mike appeared, ready to take their orders.

"Business Burgers?" he asked.

"I'm a vegetarian," Pete said.

"Had lunch," the others chorused.

"How about coffee and something sweet?" Mike said.

Looking from one to another, they settled on double lattes and biscotti.

"Decaf or regular?"

After each of the other three men said regular, Earl did the same.

The men made small-talk until their coffees came. Then Pete took the lead. "Okay, here's the plan. The first six videos can be done on campus, using tapes from this summer's project. Earl has offered to let us work out of his house for now. Les and I have creative and marketing expertise and will work on that end of the business. Doug and Earl can work on the production and business end. Agreed?"

Doug opened his briefcase, and took out four folders, and gave one to each of them. "I did some projections. They show that by this time next year we could be doing very well. In three years, we'll be rich. My estimates are based on the inquiries and commitments we've already got. Les and Pete have a plan to market directly to schools. Individuals will be sold through infomercials and the PBS shows."

Les sat forward. "Pete and I have looked at the videos closely, and they can be cut several different ways. The way they are now, each segment runs half an hour. They can be broken and reintegrated so that many careers are discussed on one tape."

"There are a few things I've realized since the original videos were made," Earl said. "I would like to add more depth to the interviews. I want to address the philosophy of work and make a separate set of tapes for an older audience."

Pete shook his head. "Whenever you add insight or depth, you eliminate part of your audience. The more bland they are, the more sales you can expect from a product like this. Do not overestimate the intelligence of the American public."

"This could be important," Earl said. "It would mean the difference between the videos being simple information and being something inspiring, transforming. I don't want to produce bland, meaningless filler material."

Les took a conciliatory tone. "I don't think you realize how good the fruits of your first efforts are. Why don't we continue to use the original formula for a few more shows? We can talk about changes later." He opened his briefcase and pulled out a plaque that said:

Earl Witherspoon
Director of Career Information
and Assessment Services

"I've found you a real office at school. This is for your door. We'll get you a teaching assistant to handle your classes this semester."

"But—" Earl started but was interrupted.

"We've got a product with a market," Pete said. "We've got projections that blow your socks off. Why mess with something that's working? I assume we all agree that money is the only legitimate way of keeping score."

Earl stared at the name plaque as the others nodded.

"Good, then we're all agreed. We've got a real winner here. I've never seen one easier to do or sell. We'll move into Earl's house next week and really start work."

After the others left, Earl took Dee's note from his pocket and read:

IT'S ONE THING TO FLIRT WITH
DESTINY, ANOTHER TO FULFILL HER

It wasn't as if he was just going to make bland videos forever—they would be used to establish the market. He would add discussions about the philosophy of work and second careers later. And maybe that wasn't such a good idea anyway. This changing the world or making-things-better stuff was kind of airy-fairy. Lots of people said so. Maybe money was all that was important. He crushed Dee's note and threw it in the waste bin as he left the restaurant.

To Divorce or Not

Rachael and Paul were standing in front of the order counter of Mike's Magic Burgers when Mike came out of the kitchen. "Hey, how are you guys? Deluxe Tropical Burgers?"

Rachael answered in a controlled voice. "No, Mike, we'll have Decision Burgers."

Mike was afraid of Rachael and thought that she and mild-mannered Paul made a very unlikely couple.

Rachael led the way to a booth in the rear of the restaurant. They sat neither looking at nor speaking to each other.

Mike delivered their food and made a hasty retreat.

The two picked up their burgers, closed their eyes, and took large bites. They opened their eyes in the reception area of what appeared to be an old government office building. "Uumph, not much of a location for a first-rate marriage counselor," Rachael said.

A mature woman with two pair of glasses—she wore one and the other hung on from a cord around her neck—sat behind a metal secretarial desk addressing envelopes on a manual Underwood typewriter. Seeing the couple, she took off the glasses she was wearing and put on the ones that had been hanging around her neck. "Can I help you?"

Rachael spoke. "We're from Mike's. We have a decision to make."

"What kind of decision is it?"

"Divorce," Rachael snapped. "We're thinking about divorce."

"I see," the receptionist said. "Room D, down the hall."

Rachael walked purposefully toward the door. Paul followed. Entering Room D, they saw an unkempt, older man. He was heavy, with thin hair; wearing a baggy suit; and sitting behind a desk like the receptionist's. "Come in. Come in. Sit down. What kind of decision do we have here?" he asked.

"Divorce," Rachael said as the two of them sat in the chairs in front of the desk.

The man turned to look at the books on the shelves and then the diplomas on the wall. "Excuse me." He stood up and walked around the room. As he did, material swatches disappeared, and large picture books shrunk and turned into books about relationships and marriage counseling. As he sat down, the certificates on the wall also changed and showed Rachael and Paul that they were in the presence of a degreed and certified marriage counselor. "There, now we're ready. What is the problem?"

Rachael started. "He never talks to me. He goes to work. He comes home. He watches television. He never talks to me. I don't know how he feels about anything—whether he loves me, or anything. He's nice enough in other ways. He helps out around the house, takes out the trash, helps with the dishes, that kind of thing, but he never talks to me. I don't know what he's thinking or feeling."

Paul looked down at his hands, folded in his lap.

The counselor addressed Paul softly. "Son, how do you feel about this? What's going on for you? Do you love this woman?"

When Paul looked up, his face was wet with tears. "I'm not good at talking. I never know what to say."

"Son, this is a magic place. All you have to do is think about your feelings and want to express what's in your heart, and it will happen."

Paul continued to stare at his hands.

Rachael fidgeted. "See, that's what he does at home too. He won't talk."

The counselor silenced her with a look. Before either of them could speak again, Paul began, mumbling,

> *How do I love thee? Let me count the ways.*
> *I love thee to the depth and breadth and height*
> *My soul can reach, when feeling out of sight*
> *For the ends of Being and ideal Grace.*

His voice was now clear. He stood with his arms outstretched and looked at Rachael,

> *I love thee to the level of everyday's*
> *Most quiet need, by sun and candle-light.*
> *I love thee freely, as men strive for Right;*
> *I love thee purely, as they turn from Praise.*
> *I love thee with the passion put to use*
> *In my old griefs, and with my childhood's faith.*

He lowered onto one knee and finished full-throated,

> *I love thee with a love I seemed to lose*
> *With my lost saints,—I love thee with the breadth,*
> *Smiles, tears, of all my life!—and, if God choose,*
> *I shall but love thee better after death.*

Then he rested his head on Rachael's lap.

"I had no idea," she said.

"I wouldn't have guessed you were an Elizabeth Barrett Browning fan," the counselor said. "But it seems to have done the trick. Nice work, son."

After they left, Mike walked in through a nearly invisible door on the side of the room. "How'd it go?"

The counselor shook his head. "Paul recited that Elizabeth Barrett Browning Sonnet."

"How do I love thee…? That one?"

"That's the one."

"Paul?"

"Yes. On bended knee."

"Paul? And Rachael, what did she do?"

"She liked it."

"Rachael?"

"She teared up."

"Rachael?"

The counselor nodded.

"Wow. That really is magic."

Chopping Onions

Mike and Destiny worked in the kitchen of Mike's Magic Burgers, preparing food for the annual party to be held that evening. "How many years have we done this?" Destiny asked.

"I'm not sure. I do know this will be the sixteenth year that the party is being held on the Friday of the regional sheriffs' convention, instead of the anniversary of the real party. We changed it so we could be certain Chet would be out of town."

"Whatever happened to the couple who got married?" Destiny said.

"This comes up every year," Mike said. "No one knows what happened to them or even remembers their names."

"Has Chet been sheriff sixteen years?" Destiny asked.

"No, but the previous sheriff, Joe, sent Chet to the

convention in his place, so he could come to the party," Mike said.

"Poor Chet—all that anger, for all these years."

Mike nodded. "How's Earl?"

"Don't know. I haven't had much time to think about anything but work. My trip was terrific. I met great people and sold a ton of books," Destiny said.

"You two haven't talked?" Mike said.

"No," Destiny said. "We keep missing each other. You know how I am when I'm working."

"Do you know he's back in his old house?" Mike said.

"Yeah."

"And that he's made a deal to produce and sell videos?" Mike said.

"Yeah."

"You haven't missed much," Mike assured Destiny.

Bubba Bronson stood in the doorway. "Destiny? Is that Destiny Robertson working in the kitchen at Mike's? Just like the old days."

"Bubba?" Destiny grabbed a towel and wiped her hands as she walked toward the large man and threw her arms around him. "I haven't seen you in ages. I've been to your store, buying books a few times, but you weren't there. You look great."

Bubba beamed. "A little heavier."

"Aren't we all?" Destiny responded.

Bubba and Mike waved to each other. Mike said, "What's up? Come to help? You can chop onions."

"Actually, I came to ask if I could bring an old friend to the party tonight," Bubba said.

Mike cringed.

"If it's a problem…"

"Hey, I want everyone to come," Mike said. "But sometimes when the magic gets going, it can be real confusing for newcomers. I won't be able to watch out for him. You'll have to be responsible."

"And there's the ejection factor," Destiny said. "The magic sometimes kicks people out."

Now Bubba looked concerned. "I forgot about that. I think he'll be okay. He's a big Swede, real gregarious, sweet fella. I've known him for years. He's a psych prof at Berkeley, and he's just written a book about the men's movement called *Turgid Members*. He's reading at the store tomorrow."

Destiny snickered. "Great title."

"We think this could be real big," Bubba said.

"Could cause the movement to swell," Mike said.

Bubba nodded.

"Here, chop." Mike set the onions and a knife in front of Bubba.

Annual Bash

Though few of the current attendees had been at the original wedding in the park, the one where Chet's grandfather died, everyone knew and repeated the story.

Bubba Bronson introduced Sven Olefson, who had a date with him—she looked twitchy. Mike whispered a reminder to keep an eye on the couple. He didn't really think Sven was going to be a problem, but his date stood out like a sore thumb. Destiny, Mike, and Dee all mentioned how familiar the woman looked, but no one had caught her name; they were too busy setting things up and figured they would talk with her later.

A couple who looked like archetypical government workers from the fifties stood eating hors d'oeuvres. He wore a baggy suit. She wore glasses and had a second pair hanging around her neck. They knew many of the people in the room.

Phil made his usual entrance and began a conversation immediately. This worked out well, since he would become comfortable enough to listen about the time other people became comfortable enough to talk.

Daphne and her assistant, Blanche (who was the person who suggested Mike's to her in the first place), were among those listening to Phil. Each had a slight look of speculation, indicating they may have a thing or two to say to him later. A large tanned man in white pants said hello to the two women, and they blushed, then laughed.

John looked fresh-scrubbed and eager when he walked in with Catherine; her great-grandmother, Estelle; and her great-grandmother's friend, Charles. (A close friend of her second husband, Lawrence, whom she met at the fateful wedding, married and then buried twenty years later. Estelle and Charles claimed they didn't marry because they liked the idea of living in sin. As Estelle put it, "After seventy-five, it takes a little extra to get ya excited," but that's another story.)

Dee stood talking with a journalism student, who was telling her about his conversations with the ghost of Lyndon Johnson and his displeasure that Lyndon refused to arrange an introduction to the ghosts of either Elvis or Jimmy Hoffa, either of whom would have been great for a book—the definitive biography of Johnson having, in the journalist's opinion, already been written.

Rachael and Paul acted like newlyweds. Paul's longtime friends were thrilled the couple had found this happiness. Longtime friends of Rachael wondered how long she would remain satisfied. Several people who didn't know them at all had bets on how long they'd stay at the party—given the impression that they needed privacy.

Hinckley and Maria were the most mismatched-looking couple, she in a gauze skirt and he in his Ralph Lauren slacks and sports jacket. But it was apparent to everyone they enjoyed each other. They were speaking with a tall androgynous person in a long white-satin cape with feathers floating in the air around it.

Other people were standing in groups of three to six, entertaining one another with tales from previous parties. Scott and Coleen were serving snacks on trays and making sure everyone mingled. Then, with a feeling like the sudden change in the barometric pressure before a big storm, the magic kicked in. Those who had been to previous parties knew what the feeling was and told the newer people not to be afraid or resist when whatever it was that was going to happen happened.

Everyone was expectant and watchful by the time Earl walked in. It seemed that everything stopped and a spotlight shone on him. Heads turned, looking to see if there were other lights and they saw one shining on the awkward woman—Sven's date. She, who seconds before, hadn't been able to decide whether to stand or sit, how to hold her hands, or what to eat. She who now walked confidently across the middle of the room toward Earl.

Seeing them, Mike, Destiny, and Dee understood why she looked familiar; she and Earl looked alike, like brother and sister, in the way long-married people dressed by one hand often do. They realized the woman must be his wife, Beth.

Destiny stood between her mother and her son-in-law, watching as Earl was led away. She turned and saw Sven try to move fast, try to yell. She saw his disappointment and averted her eyes, to give him the privacy he needed—as did everyone else except his friend Bubba, who stood at his side, telling him it would be okay, and not to struggle.

The two spotlights joined into one, and Earl and Beth followed it out the door. The pressure in the room returned to normal. Dee put her arm around Destiny, pulled her close, and asked if she was all right. Scott asked if she wanted to shoot a few baskets.

"Well, Mom, you were right. Still unfinished business there. How come I didn't see it?" Destiny saw Bubba talking to his friend and added, "You may want to talk with Sven. He looks confused. He might need some help. I'm going to shoot hoops with my son-in-law."

Darleen Hamilton, the high school coach, and Phil Martino, from the Boys & Girls Club, were already there when Destiny and Scott got to the alley behind the restaurant where a basket was mounted. The four were playing lightheartedly when Bubba and Sven came out.

Destiny looked at Sven. "Okay?"

"Little disoriented," he said.

"Exercise'll help," Destiny assured him. "Join us. We like bringing new people into the game."

After a while, the party pulled them in for dinner. The meal filled the room with the love of the universe. They played some old-time rock and roll, then the Beatles—the Sgt. Pepper album played more than once. Later they all joined hands and sang *Imagine*. Everyone tried to hug everyone else and tell them they loved them.

Eventually, the party ended, as it did every year.

Epilogue

The party was the last time Earl was seen in Mike's Magic Burgers.

He made a lot of money selling those videos—they were never changed from the original format. Beth moved back to town and took Earl's job at the high school. After the demand for career videos waned, the company diversified into exercise videos and then quilting videos. (It's more popular than most people think.) Recently they started making juicing videos. People say Earl has begun seeing Harvey again on Friday afternoons. During a recent interview on PBS, he said, "Changing the world is overrated," as if he knew what he was talking about.

Destiny stayed in town. Her daughter had twins, and she and Mike enjoy being grandparents. Lately they've started to wonder if they could be lovers again—but don't want to ruin their friendship.

Maria and Hinckley married. He left the bank and now helps her at her store. There was a lull in the sale of chicken items, so they shifted to cows. Last time I was there, the store was called Mooove Over, and it was very busy.

Daphne decorated her house using Southwestern style. You either like it or you don't. She doesn't care. It's her house.

John got his degree in mechanical engineering and has five patents. His grocery cart that can walk up stairs appears to have broad appeal. Catherine decided to go to medical school. They intend to marry.

Dee continues to read palms but lately has started to also do card readings. She continues to be eighty-three years old, though everyone else has aged.

Phil remains a delight. He and Daphne enjoy going to the desert together.

The receptionist in the Decision office got bifocals.

Even with all the bad press beef has gotten, Mike's Magic Burgers is still in business. Only people with an open heart can find it. They find a place like it, in every town.

About the Author

Rose Baldwin is a Midwesterner by birth and a Californian by choice. A retired civil servant, she lives near Palm Springs with her two cats. *Mike's Magic Burgers* is her second book. *The Claire Stories* was published October 2016. She is currently working on more stories and poems about Claire and her friends.

The book is available from Amazon.com and other retail outlets.

93428085R00119

Made in the USA
Columbia, SC
11 April 2018